Doug J. Swanson has been a newspaper reporter since 1977 and is currently on the staff of the *Dallas Morning News*. Although he's come across a lot of sleazy lawyers, rogue cops and depraved criminals in his time, he's also met those who are honest, straight and innocent.

He is the author of one previous book featuring Jack Flippo, *Big Town*, which won the Crime Writers' Association John Creasey Award for Best First Crime Novel of 1994. *Big Town* is available in paperback from Warner Books.

Doug J. Swanson lives near Dallas with his wife and family.

Also by Doug J. Swanson

BIG TOWN

DOUG J. SWANSON

Dreamboat

WARNER BOOKS

A *Warner* Book

First published in United States in 1995 by
HarperCollins Publishers, Inc.

First published in Great Britain in 1995
by Little, Brown and Company

This edition published by Warner Books in 1996

A CIP catalogue record for this book
is available from the British Library.

ISBN 0 7515 1584 1

Printed and bound in Great Britain by Clays Ltd, St Ives plc

Warner Books
A Division of
Little, Brown and Company (UK)
Brettenham House
Lancaster Place
London WC2E 7EN

The author wishes to thank the following for their time and expertise: Dick Haayen, Jim Ewell of the Dallas County Sheriff's Department, and Don Kirby of the Dallas County Medical Examiner's Office.

Special thanks also to the editors of the *Dallas Morning News* for their generous granting of time to write.

DREAMBOAT

The chief of the volunteer fire department was eating a sandwich of luncheon meat and Miracle Whip on white bread when he saw the body. It floated face down about fifty feet away. Wayne Ambrose swallowed and pointed. "We got us a winner."

The other man in the boat, a fat fishing guide known as Big Junior, turned to look. "About damn time," he said. He steered with a trolling motor as Wayne reached with a gaff. At the touch of the hook the body rolled over as if weightless.

Wayne studied a man with short dark hair, probably in his thirties, wearing jeans, a plaid shirt, gloves, and one shoe. The face was bloated, with skin the color of rancid pork. Turtles and fish had nibbled at the gray lips.

Big Junior said, "Hey, Wayne, how come you stop eatin' that sammidge?"

Another ten minutes and the sun would start to drop behind the jagged line of tall pines along the shore. Wayne took a two-way radio from a canvas bag and called the Baggett County Sheriff's Office. When the dispatcher answered, he said, "Wayne on the water. Tell the sheriff we finally got our man."

He had spent the last six afternoons at Lake Dolph Briscoe. December drownings were that way, even when the weather had been mild. You waited for bacteria to fill the body with gas, make it into a balloon. The colder the water, the slower the germs.

"Less call it a day," Big Junior said. He turned a key and started the 150-horsepower Mercury. "I done bagged my limit of stiffs."

Wayne pulled a rope through two of the dead man's belt loops and tied the ends around a starboard cleat. "Least I can get back to work now," he said.

He had closed his Fina station early every day to come out to the lake and hunt for the missing man. Baggett County, the smallest in East Texas, contained not a single person with a wetsuit and air tanks. The day after the drowning report had been filed Wayne had asked the sheriff to bring in a diver from somewhere else, let him find the body. Let's speed this search up, Wayne said. Telling the sheriff, It can't cost that much. The words had barely left Wayne's mouth before the sheriff answered no.

"All set?" Big Junior asked. Wayne finished the knot and nodded. Big Junior gave the throttle an easy pull, and the blue-spangled fiberglass boat cut through the lake's light chop. Wayne sat on a cushioned swivel chair and zipped his red Fina windbreaker against the chill.

"Hope them damn fish bite tomorrow," Big Junior said over the noise of the outboard. "Got two customers out for half a day." He glanced back toward the body. "I'll tell 'em, Boys, you wanted to catch the real big one, you ought to come yesterday."

When they reached shore the two men pulled Big Junior's boat onto its trailer, leaving the dead man to bob in the shallows, up against some reeds. Then they dragged the body onto the concrete boat ramp with Wayne using the gaff and Big Junior tugging on the rope. "This thing," Big Junior said, "smells like six tubs of bad mackerel."

Wayne found an old blue plastic shower curtain in the back of his truck, unfolded it, and covered everything, head to toe. "Appreciate the help, Big," he said. They stood about ten feet up the boat ramp as he slapped Big Junior on the shoulder.

"Time to call it a day." Big Junior wiped his hands with a rag. "Time to head for the house, have me some supper and catch the Cowboys on *Monday Night Football*. I'm gonna pop a top and . . . oh, shit." He put one hand to one unshaven jowl and stared past Wayne toward the body. "He's movin', Wayne. That boy's still alive."

Wayne whipped around to look. "Swear to God," Big Junior said. "Swear to God I seen him move." Wayne watched for a good twenty seconds and saw nothing. He was about to laugh off Big Junior when the plastic sheet stirred.

"There it is." Big Junior was talking in a hard whisper. "You see it, Wayne? I seen it. You see it?"

Wayne still had the gaff. He went to the body, hooked a corner of the shower curtain, and lifted it away. "Careful now," Big Junior said.

A sudden squirming inside the man's shirt made them

both jump. It was as if his heart were trying to force its way out of the body.

Wayne gripped the handle of the gaff. Big Junior said, "Get on back, Wayne."

Between two buttons on the corpse's wet shirt a dark space opened. The space gave way to a mouth, next an eye, and then the whole fish. It worked its way out from under the shirt and flopped a couple of times on the man's abdomen before falling with a light smack onto the boat ramp.

Wayne took a breath and relaxed. After a moment he shook his head, picked up the shower curtain, and covered the body again.

Big Junior wrapped his hand around the fish. "Not a bad-sized bass," he said as he tossed it back into the lake. "Guess that proves up one theory."

Wayne looked up from the body. "Huh?"

"Bass," Big Junior said. "Don't need live bait to catch them babies."

2 At just after ten a patrol car rolled west-
bound on Ross Avenue, pointed toward the
skyline of downtown Dallas. The December
night air was so sharp and clear that it
seemed you could almost touch the bright
bars of light that ran along the thrusts and
angles of the towering headquarters of failed banks.

From the patrol car's back seat, Jack Flippo listened to
two officers talk. Tubbs and Yancy, a couple of cops swapping tales about corpses.

"You hear about Taylor?" said Yancy. "Last week he
takes a call at Bert's Catfish House on Grand. Place is
closed up for the night, right? Bert's old lady shows up to
take him home, the door's unlocked but no Bert."

"Fun and games," said Tubbs.

"Taylor ducks inside to look around. Guess what he
finds?"

"Bert."

"In the deep freeze. Shot in the head and stuffed in the
deep freeze."

"See 'em everywhere nowadays."

"Get this. Taylor walks outside and says, Bert sleeps with the fish sticks."

Jack shifted in the back seat. The pain was becoming hard to ignore. When the two cops finished laughing Jack said, "These cuffs are too damn tight."

"Well, sir." Tubbs, a large man in his fifties, fixed Jack in the mirror. He had a brush cut that showed off the rolls of fat on the back of his head. "We're about two minutes from the jail."

Jack leaned forward to take the pressure off his wrists, shackled behind him. The patrol car turned onto Elm Street and approached Dealey Plaza and the Triple Underpass. JFK PARKING said a sign outside one lot. It had a bad painting of Kennedy's face that made him look as if his cheeks were stuffed with nuts for the winter.

The car crossed Industrial Boulevard and passed down the ramp to the garage beneath the jail. Tubbs caught Jack's eye in the mirror again. "You know the drill here, you been around enough times."

Yancy, who looked to be about two weeks out of the academy, regarded Jack for a few seconds, then faced forward. "Repeat customer?" he asked Tubbs.

"Mr. Flippo here used to be an assistant district attorney," Tubbs said. "Used to lock up the bad guys for a living."

Yancy looked at Jack again. "Don't say."

"Headed back to the old stomping grounds," Tubbs said as he parked the car. "Couldn't stay away from the place." He laid an elbow on the back of the seat and turned to address Jack. "Couldn't stay away. 'Course it probably looks different from the other side of the fence."

6

*　　*　　*

He'd had a couple of drinks, but Jack was able to stand up straight at the jail book-in desk. A woman in a blue uniform sat before a computer. She wore her hair in a tight bun, and she held her face like someone who gets fined a day's pay for smiling.

The woman typed as he answered her questions. Full name? Jackson Andrew Flippo. Age? Thirty-five. Occupation? Nonpracticing lawyer, he could have said. Or newly licensed investigator. Researcher, he told her. Height was six-one and weight, 170. Hair was blond and eyes were green. She wanted to know if he had any aliases. He had once dated a girl who called him Pookie-wookie, but he kept that to himself. No tattoos. No health problems. Any scars? she asked. Just this big one, he said, that my baby left on my heart. The typist didn't laugh.

Jack spent the next couple of hours in a holding cell, watching a guy in a Santa suit throw up on his red socks. Then it was off to a magistrate's hearing, where he was charged with simple assault. Cactus Bloodworth posted his $200 bond, and was waiting for Jack when they turned him loose.

"Jack, so you done some hard time," Cactus said. "Three, four hours in the big house."

"Thanks for coming."

"Your buddies from the bar didn't even have to phone me. Jail guard I know called me even before they did. He says, Guess who got in a fight and ended up down here. You could have knocked old Cactus over with a chicken fart, Jackie."

They walked across the street to the parking lot. "Stuff happens," Jack said.

"Don't I know it. What was it this time?"

"My ex-wife's boyfriend—"

"Say no more. Ex-wife, the magic word, Hey, the good Lord gave Job what—boils? He should've thrown in an ex-wife."

They reached Cactus's Jaguar and got in. Cactus drove down Industrial as he described the trials of having three former Mrs. Bloodworths. Jack had heard it all several times before. It always touched on the cost of new cars and breast implants.

Before he had changed it, Cactus's real name had been Curtis Bruce. He was an ex-private investigator, now a lawyer, who had lost an eye in a car wreck, which through a decade of mythmaking had become a shootout with a Jamaican drug posse. Cactus had a black patch now and wore his long silver hair Buffalo Bill–style. He liked to sit in bars with pretty women and talk about writing a screenplay based on his life, called *One Private Eye*. Rivals said *One Public Dick* was more like it.

He might be easy to laugh at, but he pulled in the business. Although he no longer did the work himself, he still got a good number of private investigation jobs. He tossed most of them Jack's way. Cactus would tell Jack, You're the man, you're the only one can handle this case, old Cactus is trusting you completely on this one, and don't forget my 25 percent rake.

"About to call you anyway," Cactus said, pulling his Jag into a Denny's. "I got a job for you. Let's grab a cup of coffee and talk about it."

When they had settled into a booth, Cactus studied his reflection in the back of a spoon. He smoothed his full silver mustache and said, "Got a client that's been with me a long, long time, Jack. Continental Centurion, an insurance company out of Kansas City. Anything they have in the Southwest, they call old Cactus first. You know why?"

Jack looked at the plastic-coated pictures of food on the menu. He felt like an alley cat after a night of crawling in and out of garbage cans.

"You know why?" Cactus said again.

Jack used a napkin to wipe the remains of county ink from his fingertips. "Why?"

"'Cause they want the job done fast and they want it done right. They want it done Cactus-style. Now, they phoned me yesterday about a case in East Texas, place called Baggett. Some old boy drowned down there last week with a half-million policy on him. The company needs someone to drive down and sniff around a little, make sure everything's on the square."

"I can drive and sniff."

"I'd do it myself, just for old times' sake, 'cause it's a quick hit for good pay, but old Cactus is leaving town tomorrow. I'm seeing people in L.A., then I'm taking my ladyfriend to Ha-wah-yah for a week. Has this stallion gone crazy?"

"Sounds nice."

"Has this old bobcat lost his mind?"

"What's her name?"

"Who?"

"The lady," Jack said. "The one you're taking to Hawaii."

"Twenty-two years old, Jack, you oughta see her. Works out every day and says she has a thing for one-eyed

9

rich men. Last night, she's got me in bed, she's doing all the right things, I mean she's riding me like a thoroughbred. Old Cactus might as well have been chained to the mattress. You know what I mean."

"Not lately," Jack said.

"Then she stops right in the middle and tells me, baby, let's get married in Maui. On the beach, at sunset. How do you like that?"

Jack laughed. "You're gonna do it, aren't you?"

"The price of doing monkey business," Cactus said.

"Well, enjoy yourself. I'll stay here and work the East Texas job."

"Like I said, drive on out to wherever the hell this place is and poke around, see if you find any dog shit. And Jack? Just write it up. Don't step in it."

Wednesday night Jack unfolded his Texas map and found the town of Baggett, population 3,412, seat of Baggett County, about 125 miles east of Dallas. The next morning before sunrise he pulled himself from bed, climbed into his Ford pickup truck, and drove. He turned on the radio, thinking about modern marvels: A guy tells a fart joke in New York, and someone fifteen hundred miles away can hear it at the same time.

Jack traveled the freeway against the commute. Hundreds of pairs of headlights blew past him, a three-lane meteor shower, as he rolled between look-alike subdivisions and strip shopping centers. Squat buildings with giant signs, mile after mile. The first hint of dawn was a fading of the sky behind a MacFrugal's store.

He hit the ragged outskirts and finally the countryside, which didn't have much in the way of scenic beauty unless you counted mobile home dealerships. The fields were bare and full of puddles. The day stayed overcast and chilly, the way the end of the year was supposed to be.

Just past Sulphur Springs Jack left the interstate and took a smooth farm-to-market road with little traffic. About fifty miles from Baggett he stopped for a bitter cup of coffee and reread his notes.

Continental Centurion Associates wanted to know about the death of one Mingo Gideon, thirty-three, who had been missing for six days when his body floated to the surface of Lake Dolph Briscoe. The next morning a man named Rex Echols had filed a policy claim.

Mingo Gideon and Rex Echols owned a bar in Dallas, the Melon Patch Ranch. Six months ago Rex had purchased partner's insurance from Continental Centurion. Mingo's death would pay Rex $500,000.

"Go on down there and see if anything looks screwy," Cactus had told Jack. "Shouldn't take long, a couple days in the boonies, that's about it. I'll spring for a night in a motel. Eat some greasy food, hump a small-town girl if you want, get the straight tale, come on home."

As Jack neared Baggett the land changed. The trees grew bigger and the brush thicker. Oaks canopied the highway in places. There were pine forests, red dirt, and hills, which meant he had entered East Texas. His map wouldn't say it, but he had crossed the border into Dixie.

Baggett had a sawmill and a state school for the retarded. The high school football team was called the Bandits. A billboard proclaimed that the Bandits had been state 2-A champs in 1981. The town wasn't big enough for a McDonald's, but it was blessed by a Dairy Queen. The Lions Club put up a sign welcoming Jack and everyone else arriving by highway.

His first stop was the courthouse, a three-story block

of red brick and gray limestone at the center of the town square. A statue of a Confederate soldier stood on the patch of lawn. Jack parked across the street, in front of a video rental store with a cardboard cutout of Whitney Houston in the window. The New South.

He climbed the courthouse stairs to the top floor and walked down a hallway overhung by stammering, buzzing fluorescent lights. Black letters on a door's frosted glass said SHERIFF'S OFFICE. Below that, LOYCE SLAPP, SHERIFF.

Jack went in and found a grandmotherly woman at a desk with a phone and a radio control board. He told her he wanted to see this Loyce Slapp, if he could, please. He got himself ready for a sheriff with a beer gut and a butch haircut, all tobacco juice and attitude, a badass old boy.

The woman said, "Sheriff's over at Sir Tans-a-lot right now."

Jack nodded.

"The one acrosst the square," she said, "not the one on the highway. He should be back in about ten minutes, you'd like to wait. I'd call him for you but Sheriff don't like to have his sessions interrupted."

"I can wait." Jack sat in a gray metal folding chair and read an old copy of *Sports Afield* while the woman worked a crossword puzzle.

Ten minutes later the door opened and the woman said, "Here he is."

Sheriff Loyce Slapp stood about five-six and probably weighed 145 pounds, counting clothes. Be hard for him to sue for libel, Jack thought, if the local rag ever called him Pee-Wee.

The sheriff wore a khaki uniform starched to armor-

13

plate. He had black hair gelled straight back and mud-colored narrow eyes that looked Jack up and down without giving away anything. His skin was Hollywood bronze. He put Jack in mind of a ferret with a two-picture deal.

When Jack introduced himself, Loyce Slapp waited a few seconds before pointing toward the next room. His office floor was spotless gleaming linoleum and the walls bare institutional green. The top of the sheriff's gray metal desk had a calendar, a telephone, a phone book, a pad and pencil, a nameplate, and nothing else. After Jack told him why he had come, Loyce Slapp started to speak, talking in a voice so quiet and toneless that Jack had to lean forward to hear.

"... have to say I was expecting someone like you when I learned the amount of insurance money involved."

"Who told you about the insurance?" Jack asked.

"Word gets around."

"So a lot of people know about this?"

"I didn't say that." The sheriff folded his hands on the desk. He had lacquered nails.

"People chattering about this at the cafe?" Jack said. "That sort of thing?"

"I didn't say that, either."

Jack took a breath and regrouped. The sheriff, his face suddenly troubled, pulled a shiny black wallet from his pocket.

He counted his bills twice, then paged through the thin phone book.

"Sheriff, what I need from you—" Jack stopped when Loyce Slapp picked up his phone and dialed.

"This is Sheriff Slapp," he said into the phone, talking like a television golf announcer before a big putt. "How many minutes did you charge me for today? . . . That's what I thought you did, why I'm calling. I never stay in for twenty, you know that. Twenty minutes and I burn, and I don't like to burn. I go to fifteen and that's it."

Jack watched him drum the desktop lightly with his varnished nails. "You know why?" the sheriff said to the phone. "Take a guess . . . That's right, twenty minutes and I burn. And after that I peel. How do you think that looks?" Loyce Slapp picked up his pencil and did some figuring on his pad. "Two dollars and forty-five cents you owe me, plus sales tax . . . No, bring it over to my office."

He hung up and looked at Jack. "Are we finished?"

"I want to see your department's report on the drowning."

"Copies cost fifteen cents each."

"And I'd like to talk to your investigator who worked the case."

"You already are."

"You worked it."

The sheriff nodded once as he opened the lap drawer to his desk.

"Why is that?" Jack asked.

Loyce Slapp found a piece of paper in the drawer without searching and handed it to Jack. It was one page, neatly typed. The complainant was Mingo Neal Gideon, white male. Nature of incident: Body in lake. Reported by: Baggett Fire. Time: 4:00 P.M. Date: 12-6. Filed by: L. Slapp.

Jack read the narrative out loud: "Baggett Fire Chief Ambrose advised body recovered in Lake Dolph Briscoe.

ID found on body. Justice of Peace notified." He placed the paper on the sheriff's desk. "That's it?" Jack asked. "That's all you've got?"

The sheriff returned the paper to his drawer. "How much they paying you, this insurance company?" He asked it as if he were inquiring about where Jack bought his shoes. "They paying you by the question?"

"I'd like to know how Mingo Gideon came to be in that lake, number one. Number two, I'd be interested in the names of any witnesses. Number three, I want to see the autopsy report."

Jack waited. Thinking, I'm looking at a guy whose heart pumps cold grease. Loyce Slapp stared back, then reached into his desk drawer and found another sheet of paper. He inspected it before letting Jack have it. "This is the supplemental report."

It said Mingo Gideon, Rex Echols, and someone named Bobby Slater had been fishing in the lake. They returned to shore and drank beer for an hour. Around midnight Mingo took the boat out by himself and didn't come back.

"No one saw him fall overboard?" Jack said. "We don't know why he went in the water?"

"It was dark."

Jack pointed to the paper. "Who's this Bobby Slater?"

"Fishing buddy, I suppose."

"Do you have a phone number for him?"

"I look like the phone company?"

"Who has the autopsy?"

Loyce Slapp put the supplemental report back in his

drawer. "You'll have to talk to Webb Carroll about that. Our Justice of the Peace."

"Where's he?"

The sheriff picked up his phone and dialed. "Let's see can you catch him before he goes home for his nap."

Justice of the Peace Webb Carroll's office was on the first floor of the courthouse, down the hall from the district clerk. A soft drink vending machine guarded the entrance. Jack walked in and saw a man in his sixties, with thin colorless hair parted in the middle. His eyes were a watery blue, his nose a wreck of spidery purple veins.

Webb Carroll stood no taller than Loyce Slapp, but probably weighed seventy-five pounds more. He wore a burgundy suit gone shiny at the elbows, and played with a model train. On the floor next to his desk an old toy poodle slept on a dirty pillow.

"Look here," Webb Carroll said when he glimpsed Jack. "Just got the locomotive yesterday by UPS." He watched the train follow a track on a table next to the desk. "It's a antique Lionel. It's somethin', you think?"

"Sure is," Jack said.

"Yessir, it's somethin'. Idn't it?"

He looked at Jack, waiting for a response.

"It's something," Jack said.

Webb Carroll smiled. "Sure is."

The track threaded its way through a setting of miniature buildings and six-inch trees. There was a park, and a lake of painted blue. Tiny figures enjoyed a picnic lunch on a small square of checkered cloth. It looked like a clean, wholesome town that didn't mind a freight train constantly running through it.

After a while Webb Carroll said, "What can I do for you?"

Jack mentioned Continental Centurion, and said he would like to see the report on Mingo Gideon.

"Too bad about him," Webb Carroll said. "But, hey, at least he didn't leave his partner high and dry."

"What do you mean?"

Webb Carroll laughed. "You're askin' me? That's a good one."

He leaned over and spoke to the sleeping poodle. "Listen to that, Jim Dandy. Comes all the way from Dallas and he's askin' me."

"So you heard about it before I got here."

"Rex weren't makin' no secret of it."

"You know Rex?"

Webb Carroll walked slowly to a gray metal file cabinet. "Everybody knows Rex. He's had a vacation house here for a while. Nice place."

"What did Rex say about the insurance?"

Webb Carroll opened the drawer and peered into the files. "Hell, I forget. I was watchin' the girls and drinkin' a toddy. Ask the sheriff, he was there."

"He was where?"

Webb Carroll turned and looked at Jack with a face that couldn't believe these questions. "At the Melon Patch Ranch. At Rex's place in Dallas. It was the second Thursday."

"The second Thursday," Jack repeated.

"You know, son ..." Webb Carroll took a sheet of paper from a file, went behind his desk, and sat down heavily in a squeaky chair. "I don't mean to be rude or nothin', but I don't see what any of these questions has to do with anything."

"Indulge me," Jack said. "What happens on the second Thursday?"

"That," Webb Carroll said, as if explaining something to a child, "is Baggett Law Enforcement Night at the Melon Patch Ranch. Free drinks."

Jack was about to ask another question when Webb Carroll handed him the piece of paper he had been holding. "Here's the report you wanted."

Like the sheriff's, this one gave Mingo's age, race, and place of death. A wallet with a driver's license and $103 in cash was recovered from the body. At the bottom of the page, above Webb Carroll's signature, was the handwritten notation, "Official determ. of cause accid. drown."

"What about the autopsy?" Jack said.

Webb Carroll watched the little train go around. It passed the station and whistled twice. "Weren't none."

Jack waited until the man looked back at him, then stared into bloodshot blue eyes. Webb Carroll said, "Hey, you know how much it costs the county when we send a body to the pathologist in Tyler? Hell, it costs us bettern ninety dollars just to ship him there and back. And that's before they start cuttin' him up."

"A dead man floats to the surface of a lake, no witnesses, and you don't order an autopsy?"

"You act like I didn't look the body over." Webb Carroll stood, leaned across his desk, and pointed a trembly finger at a line on the report after the words "visible wounds." He asked Jack, "What's it say right there?"

"It doesn't say anything."

"Exactly. 'Cause there weren't none."

Jack said, "You know, I feel like any minute now Allen Funt's going to walk in and tell me to smile." He folded the report in half and put it on the desk. "Why didn't you order toxicology?"

Webb Carroll talked to the poodle again. "Now, Jim Dandy, the dumb old country boy is supposed to say, What's that? And the top cat from the big city, he's supposed to say, It's tests for poison and drugs. And then the top cat from Dallas rolls his eyes and thinks to himself, Lord have mercy, what a bunch of hicks."

He pushed his chair back and moved to the train table, where he adjusted the picnic scene. "You want to know did he get poisoned. I'd say he got poisoned with lake water."

Jack wondered what kind of surprise he was in for next. "You photographed the scene and the body?"

Webb Carroll moved a tree to the other side of town. "'Course I did."

"I'd like to see them."

"Soon as I develop 'em, you'll be the first to know."

This time Jack had to laugh. "It's been more than a week."

"We sent the, uh, the what-you-call-it off to Houston for repair. Can't develop till we get it back."

Now Jack couldn't do anything but shake his head.

Webb Carroll watched him, then said, "What you want me to do, take the film down to the drugstore?"

"Somebody in town must have a lab you can use."

"Just take it on down to the drugstore? Like I did one time, on a car-wreck investigation? Guess what happened. Miss Minnie Weldon, sixty-seven years old, member of the First Baptist church, she's in the lab and gets the roll. She seen these pictures of dead people laid out on the highway, she liked to have a stroke right there."

Jack figured he'd reached the end of the road with Webb Carroll. He capped his pen.

"What I'm tellin' you, she liked to keel over on the spot." Webb Carroll watched the train. "We sure don't want that again, do we? Do we now?"

Jack wasn't sure if Webb Carroll was asking him or the poodle.

After lunch Jack went to the Earl D. Yost Funeral Home, a pint-sized Mount Vernon on the north side of Baggett. A hearse was parked out front, nose toward the street, ready for business.

Earl D. Yost told Jack hello, come in, of course he'd be happy to talk, have a seat, call me Earl. Earl wore a dark suit and had small-town-anchorman hair. He said he was just back from vacation in Florida, and what a time they had. The Magic Kingdom, EPCOT, and MGM. Also, Reptile World. Jack interrupted with a question about Mingo Gideon. Wait here, Earl told him, and left the office.

Jack got up from a comfortable chair and read a type-written poem that had been framed and hung above Earl's neatly arranged desk. It was called "The Funeral Director."

Our numbered days on this sweet Earth
Amount to but a few.
We laugh, we love and then we pass,
Gone like the morning dew.

And when it comes, that time to go,
Let us be proud to say
A friend was there to close our eyes
And send us on our way.

At the bottom of the page was a signature, Rex Echols.

"Here we go," Earl said as he walked back through the door, carrying an urn.

"Rex Echols wrote this?" Jack pointed to the poem.

"What a talent, that man."

Jack watched Earl take a cork coaster from a drawer, set it on the desktop, and place the urn on it. Earl said, "The cremains of Mister Mingo Gideon."

"You're joking."

"Not in the funeral business."

While Earl pulled some papers from a file cabinet, Jack studied the urn, brass with engraved filigrees. A decorated bucket of bones.

Earl sat at his desk with the papers in front of him. "Well now. What can I tell you?"

"When was the body cremated?"

"We took care of that on, let's see, December the sixth."

Jack checked his earlier notes. "But that's the same day they found it."

Earl showed a professional smile. "We have the only crematory in the tri-county area."

"On the same day the body turned up? Even in a town as colorful as this," Jack said, "I find that unusual."

Earl preserved the smile. "The family's wishes."

"No funeral, just toss him in the oven."

Now Earl put on a sober face. "As I said, the family . . ."

"They called you and said to do it now."

Earl cleared his throat. "See, the way it worked, Rex Echols spoke with the bereaved and conveyed their desires to me."

"So you never talked to them."

Earl shook his head.

"You just did what Rex Echols told you."

"He spoke with the family."

"Where do they live?"

"Now that I don't know," Earl said.

"What's it cost?" Jack asked. "The cremation, this urn, what's the tab?"

"We have some very attractive payment plans."

Jack fixed him with a stare. "C'mon, Earl."

Earl waved a hand at the papers on his desk. "Well, I don't have the invoice in front of me. Rough estimate?" Earl pursed his lips, tilted his head, and looked toward the ceiling. "I'd say eight hundred dollars, plus any subsequent temporary interment charge."

Jack tapped his pencil against the pad on his lap. "You did this eight-hundred-dollar piece of business before Mingo Gideon's survivors could send you a check. Did the business and hoped they'll pay you?" He glanced around the office, where everything had been dusted and nothing was out of place. "I think you're more careful than that, Earl."

Earl plucked some invisible lint from the monogrammed sleeve of his crisp white shirt. "Mr. Echols handled everything."

"You said that already."

"I'll never forget." Earl leaned back in his chair and pressed his hands together like a child praying. "The day he was here Mr. Echols told me, 'Earl, Mingo Gideon was like a brother to me.' He said, 'Earl, I want it handled right, and I want it handled with taste.' He said, 'Earl, I want it done with class, the way Rex Echols does everything.' I told him, 'Mr. Echols, you've come to the right place.'"

After a moment Jack said, "And?"

Earl shrugged slightly. "He said, 'I know that, Earl, I know that.' Then he paid me in cash. It was his way of, you know, helping the grieving family out."

To reach Lake Dolph Briscoe, Jack drove a two-lane through a pine forest. He passed an occasional bait shop and small grocery, but got far enough into the woods that Baggett, six miles away, seemed like a city. Instead of billboards he saw a few white crosses with some handpainted Bible verses, end-of-the-world stuff from Ephesians and Revelation. Speed limit signs were pocked with holes from shotgun pellets.

The county recreational area, a couple of miles off the highway, wasn't much more than a boat ramp, a few picnic shelters, and a wooden dock. The small asphalt parking lot was empty except for cigarette butts and flattened beer cans. Jack walked onto the dock and stood amid leavings of rusty hooks and dry, hard fish scales.

The lake's far shore was about half a mile away, he guessed. Jack stayed on the dock fifteen or twenty minutes and saw only two boats crossing in the gray, choppy distance. If someone drowned out here in the middle of a winter night, Jack thought, he could have done it without many people watching.

*   *   *

He made one last stop in Baggett. Wayne Ambrose, chief of the volunteer fire department, owned a Fina station a block off the courthouse square. Wayne was in his late twenties, with curly brown hair and good teeth. He had a tire gauge in his front pocket and pictures of his children behind the cash register.

"Lake Dolph Briscoe's not that old," Wayne said. "They built the dam about ten years ago. So when we get a drowning we can't drag the lake. Try to do that and you hang up on tree stumps all day."

"You get a good look at the body?"

"I didn't inspect it or nothing. Me and Big Junior Wilson secured it, radioed the sheriff, and headed on in. About a half-hour later Webb Carroll got there."

"He have his poodle with him?"

"Talking to that dog the whole time. Got it in the crook of his arm and telling it, 'Oh, look at this, Jim Dandy, ain't it a shame.'"

"Then what?"

"Webb got his camera out, and I went over to my truck to pack my stuff. Wasn't twenty minutes later Sheriff Slapp rolled up with Mr. Echols and another man in the patrol car."

Jack took a bag of salted peanuts from a display box on the counter and gave Wayne a dollar. "All of them in the sheriff's car," Jack said. "Slapp, Rex Echols, and who's the third guy?"

Wayne made change from the cash register. "Mr. Echols brought him over to me, first thing, and introduced him. Bobby something, I think."

"Slater?"

"That sounds about right."

"What's he look like?"

Wayne let out a breath. "You know, I wasn't paying that much attention." He looked at Jack. "Your age, I'd say. Six feet tall, maybe, little more. Had on a black ball cap, coat, gloves, all that."

Jack opened the bag of nuts. "You friends with Rex?"

"He's bought some gas here from time to time, that's about it." A car had pulled in next to the pumps. Wayne went out, tended to it, and came back in wiping his hands on a red rag. "What else for you?" he said.

Jack asked if Wayne had ever been to a Baggett Law Enforcement Night at the Melon Patch. "What the heck's that?" Wayne said.

"So you're all there at the lake," Jack said. "You and the sheriff and Bobby Slater and Rex Echols and Webb Carroll with his poodle. What happens next?"

"First Mr. Echols introduces this Bobby to Webb Carroll, and we all walk over to the body. Mr. Echols stands over it and says, 'Mingo Gideon, you poor son of a buck.' Then he says, 'Take a good look, Bobby. It's the last we'll see of Mingo Gideon. Mingo's on the bus to Jesus's house now.' Then he put his hat over his heart and started singing."

Jack waited. "He did," Wayne said. "Some song about doves in a hurricane. Tell you the truth, I don't think any of us was listening too good. The smell of the body was a little strong. Soon as Mr. Echols finished we all walked up the boat ramp to the parking lot."

"And that was all?" Jack said. Cases like this one made you expect funny business every time you opened a door. "Nothing else happened?"

"Nothing I can think of." Wayne straightened a chewing gum display. "Unless you mean, you know, just some talk I heard before I left."

"That'll do."

"Well, Mr. Echols and his friend, this Bobby, was talking while I was on the other side of my truck filling out my fire department activity report. They couldn't see me but I could hear them."

"Yeah?"

"Mr. Echols says to his friend, 'You know once in Las Vegas I saw two magicians make a whole elephant disappear?' And Mr. Echols's friend says, 'So?' And Mr. Echols says, 'You ain't even that big.'"

5 "Speak up, Sheriff. Can't hear a damn word." Rex Echols sat in his office at the Melon Patch Ranch in Dallas, talking on the phone. "His name was what? Flippo? What the hell kind of name is that?"

Sheriff Loyce Slapp didn't know. "Who'd he talk to?" Rex asked. The sheriff said he had told Rex already.

"Tell me again," Rex demanded. "A little louder this time." He visited with me, Loyce Slapp said, then the Justice of the Peace and then the fire chief. And one of the deputies saw him driving out toward the lake.

"Lotta money hangin' fire here, you know." Rex pulled his boots from his desk and sat up straight. "All right. Good job, Sheriff. I appreciate the notice. I knew they'd send some squirrel around sooner or later. The body's not even cold and they got the bloodhounds out."

Just thought I'd give you a heads-up, Loyce Slapp said.

"Appreciate the heck out of it," Rex told him. "Good to

know a man like you is on the job." Rex wondered if he could get off the line before the sheriff started dropping hints. He was about to say see you next time when Loyce Slapp mentioned he was feeling kind of lonesome.

Rex wanted to answer, Hey, welcome to the club, it's a great big old Hank Williams world out there. But all Rex said was, "Sure am sorry to hear that."

Loyce Slapp said it again, added that he could use some company. Like I don't have a business to run, Rex thought, even if it was a Thursday night. "Tell you what," Rex said. "You comin' into Dallas? Call me when you get here, let me know where you are, and I'll see we can't fix something up."

The sheriff said he would be in later this week at the Knight's Rest Inn outside Mesquite, just like always.

"Nice place," Rex said. "No charge for extra shower mold and the first ten flea bites is on the house." Loyce Slapp was silent. "Hey, Sheriff, just jokin'," Rex said. "Just had to raise a little hell. At the Melon Patch Ranch, we raise it like it was a crop."

Who will you be sending, Loyce Slapp wanted to know. "Lemme check the menu," Rex said. He looked at the clipboard hanging above his desk, ran his finger down the list of names. "I got a treat for you, Sheriff. I got Marie."

The sheriff wasn't sure. "Hey," Rex said, "Marie can't start you up, forget the motel and go check into the morgue." Loyce Slapp said he didn't want a colored girl. Rex rubbed his eyes and wished he were in Nashville writing songs. Telling himself, Life's not supposed to be this hard. Then thinking, Wait a minute, could be a song in that: *Your sweet softness saves my hard life.* He scribbled it on the back of an envelope. *You sweep away the stress and the strife.* Rex said into the phone, "Sheriff, Marie's white as you or me."

Loyce Slapp said he didn't want Marie, now that he'd thought about it. *When you're not with me it cuts like a knife.* Rex thought for a moment, then added, *You're the reason I'm leavin' my wife.* Got to be a hit, it seemed to Rex.

What he'd prefer, Loyce Slapp said, was April. Just like last time.

"April's the cream of the crop here, Sheriff. I hate to send her out, because she's the class of the Melon Patch. When she's not here the people complain. I mean, the customers come right up and ask me, Rex, where's the girl with the tattoos on her boobs?"

Send April on out to the Knight's Rest, Loyce Slapp said, and everything would be fine.

Rex went to the showroom, stood by the back wall, and counted the house, which didn't take long. He wished for a busfull of Shriners like a Dust Bowl farmer praying for rain. Some nights it didn't even pay to open the doors.

The Melon Patch Ranch squatted on Northwest Highway between 4-A Furniture Rental and Karl's Brake & Muffler Repair, not right in the Love Field flight path but close enough to hear the jets if the music was off. The building was one-story concrete block with a flat roof. Before Rex bought the place, it had housed a Mexican dance club.

Rex had owned it for almost two years, and in the first six months he thought he'd drawn the hand to put him forever in the big boys' tax bracket. There were crowds in the afternoon, crowds at night. Some days he thought he might need a wheelbarrow to haul off the cash. People in Dallas liked a no-cover place with cold beer, a good country jukebox, and friendly girls who didn't mind shaking a little tail.

He did so well he bought a house in North Dallas, along with some land in East Texas, where he put up a vacation home. Married a nineteen-year-old waitress of his with a body you saw in the magazines. Started dreaming seriously about constructing his own country music recording studio. He'd call it Echolsound.

Rex also decided to do a live act. He built a stage and took out a loan for sound and light systems. Before he bought the Melon Patch he had spent twenty years with weekend country bands, probably had been in every honky-tonk and bowling alley lounge in Texas and Oklahoma, playing George Jones and Conway Twitty knockoffs. But the Melon Patch gave Rex a chance to do what he'd always wanted: perform the songs that he wrote himself.

So every night at eight, Rex had taken the stage at the Melon Patch, where he strummed his guitar and sang his songs, like "He Done Her Dirty So His Wife Took Him to the Cleaners." A dream come true for Rex.

About the time he started his solo gig, the crowds began to fall off. Rex couldn't understand it. He'd sit in his office and try to figure why. Maybe because the neighborhood had turned a little rougher. Maybe it was the big new place a mile away, with giant-screen TVs showing sports.

The lowest point came when he couldn't make the payments anymore on his sound system and the repo man showed up. Without a quick hit of big money, the same thing would soon happen to his two houses and the Melon Patch.

Wouldn't be long, though, before he could pay everything off. Pay it all off, and buy an even better sound system. Class up his act that much more. Start planning Echolsound again. That was the reason, standing at the bar and looking at the empty tables, he now said to April, "Come on back and see me for a minute."

She said, "Soon as I get a drink for a customer." Rex went to his office and waited at his desk. Ten minutes later April arrived. Rex looked at his watch. "Shit, how long's it take to serve a drink?"

"The customer wanted to talk," April said. She wore the Melon Patch Ranch uniform, a silver bikini top and skimpy white shorts thin enough that even in dim light you could see the black thong beneath. "He wanted to talk and he had the ticket—a twenty-dollar bill. So we talked about which one he liked best." She cradled a breast in each hand and looked down on them. "He couldn't decide between the yellow rose or the red one."

"Remember that sheriff friend of mine from East Texas?"

April still stared at her tattooed flowers, which seemed to sprout from the bikini cups. "Sure. Him and me's partied a few times."

"He wants to see you one night this week."

She dropped her breasts and screwed up her face. "I don't know, Rex . . . "

"Hey, what're you making with ten people out there? On a weekday night and it's probably gonna be rainin'. You gonna make two hunnerd? Go see the sheriff and there's two hunnerd in it for you."

"He's okay," April said. "A little funny, though. Always whisperin'. He goes, April, I'm the county sheriff back in Baggett, and that's a big deal. I'm the law there. He always whispers me that, then he says, But there's a part of me that's just got to have you."

"I think I know which part," Rex said.

After April left his office he sat at his desk, trying to dodge the potholes in the books, when a waitress came in to say a customer was using a stolen credit card. Rex opened a desk drawer that held a roll of pennies and a nine-millimeter automatic. He took the pennies, then retrieved his straw cowboy hat from the top of a file cabinet. "Tell Darnell to get his ass back here," he said.

Darnell was a large black man, an ex-semipro football player, who wore his hair like Little Richard. He talked to himself a lot and liked to read books about UFOs. Rex kept him near the front door to pick off the underage and the deadbeats.

When Darnell showed up Rex told him, "We got a troublemaker. Wait in the hallway."

Rex went to the showroom. The man passing the bad card was a chubby bald guy with glasses and a baggy suit. He sat alone and tried to touch every girl who walked by.

"Give me his ticket," Rex said to the waitress. The man's tab was $29.75. "Who's got the card?" She handed it to him.

"Go on over to his table," Rex told her, "ask him does he want another drink, give him a good look at your titties. Then go on back to the dressing room."

Rex watched her do it and walked to the table.

"You like her?" Rex said.

"I think I'm in love." The man stared as she walked away.

"Want to come on back and meet her?"

"You can do that?"

"Hell, I'm the owner. I can do what I want, long's I'm keeping my good customers happy." Rex stuck out his hand. "What do you say?"

The man hesitated for a second before pumping Rex's arm like a country cousin just off the Greyhound. "I say let's go."

"See that door she just used?" Rex said. "Let's me and you head the same way."

"You don't have to ask twice." They crossed the showroom with the man in front and walked through the doorway. Darnell met them in the hall. "Which way?" the man asked.

Darnell, big enough to fill up the hallway, shook his head and smiled. Rex moved next to the man and grasped his arm. The stupid grin fell away.

"Let's have your wallet." Rex held out a palm. "Find out who you really are."

The sweat on the man's forehead gleamed in the light of the bare bulb above him. Nothing about him moved now except for his eyes, which went from Rex to Darnell and back again. "Well," Rex said. "Here's the problem every chicken faces: Lay eggs or hit the skillet."

Darnell said, "Man coming in for a landing."

Rex offered his palm again. The man didn't move or speak. His scared eyes, cartoon bugouts behind the thick glasses, were fixed on Darnell now. "We're wasting time," Rex said. "Hold him, Darnell."

Darnell put one hand against the man's neck and pushed him to the wall. Rex pulled a brown leather wallet from the man's rear pocket. The driver's license identified him as Ralph T. Duncan, age forty-four. The Visa card belonged to a Morris Morgan.

"Now are you Ralph," Rex asked, "or are you Morris? Personally, I wouldn't have either one of them names."

Darnell laughed. Rex studied the photograph on the license. "I've examined the evidence," he said, "and you look like Ralph to me. Now, Ralphie, what you have to understand is they got machines now that lets us know when somebody's using a hot card."

Ralph tried to talk. Rex leaned against the wall and spoke into his ear. "What do you think Visa tells me to do with charges on a stolen card? You think they reimburse me, don't you?"

Ralph shook his head as much as he could.

"He thinks they reimburse me, Darnell. Like life's a big carnival and somebody give Ralphie a free pass." Rex waved toward the fire exit at the end of the hall. "Get him outta here."

Darnell grabbed the back of Ralph's collar and pulled. "I've got cash," Ralph said. "I'll pay. Please." Rex took all the money from Ralph's wallet, two twenties and a single, and followed them out.

A streetlamp coated the alley with green light. Stacks

of wet cardboard boxes leaned against the building and a dumpster overflowed with trash. The night's rain had stopped, but water still dripped from a downspout. Rex shivered as he walked outside. "Good golly, it's gettin' cold. Is it supposed to ice over tonight, Darnell? You heard? How about you, Ralphie? When we finish here, I'm goin' back in and turn on Troy Dungan, see what the forecast is."

Ralph's collar was still in Darnell's grip. "Please don't kill me," Ralph said to Rex.

"Kill you." Rex laughed. "Kill you? Shit. What are we, the Mafia? We don't kill no one at the Melon Patch Ranch unless they die of a good time." He tossed the wallet into a dirty puddle at Ralph's feet. "I took forty-one dollars. That'll cover drinks plus tip."

"That's fine," Ralph said quickly.

"No, we don't kill no one," Rex said, "but I would like to pleasure you with a song which I wrote myself. Now hold onto him, Darnell." Rex began to sing.

> *Yes, I have strayed, and now you want to know why.*
> *You might as well ask why there's birds in the sky.*
> *There's just something in me that wants to leave home.*
> *I'm a rambler and a gambler and a scamp on the roam.*

"What do you think?" Rex asked.

"It's, it's real good," Ralph said, nodding fast.

"I appreciate that. Now . . ." Rex put his hand in his pocket and wrapped his fingers around the roll of pennies. "You got him, Darnell?"

"Good rockin' tonight," he answered. "Texas toast."

Well, Rex thought, Darnell's tuned to lunar radio again. No matter, because he stood behind Ralph, holding each of the man's hands by the wrist.

"That'll do her," Rex said. He pulled his fist from his pocket and swung toward Ralph's midsection, putting his weight into it and coming in hard. The flesh seemed to collapse around Rex's hand, like hitting a feather pillow.

Ralph buckled with the sound of the gut-punched. Darnell let go of his wrists. The chubby man fell on his face. He rolled over and moaned. His mangled, black-framed glasses lay beside his head on the pavement like a dead bird. Rex said, "That boy dropped like a big sack full of wet table scraps."

Darnell studied the heap at his feet. "World of hurt now."

"Here's the chorus," Rex said. "Y'all ready?" He sang,

All the bodies to touch, all the lips to be kissed,
So many temptations that I can't resist.
It hurts to admit it, but one thing I do know.
If cheatin' was a fel'ny, I'd live on Death Row.

"Thank you," Rex said as Darnell applauded. "Thank you kindly."

6 "I am very unhappy with you," the former Mrs. Jack Flippo said, and not for the first time. "I am really, really mad."

Jack had seen her staring bullets at him as he followed the waiter across the room to her table. She laid into him while he took his seat, firing all barrels before he could get the napkin unfolded and into his lap. "What'd I do?" Jack said, giving her a palms-up shrug and an innocent look. "I mean, besides the usual."

"Don't act stupid with me."

Jack wanted to say, Who needs to act? Instead he smiled a little. "Honest, Kathy," he lied, "I don't know what you're talking about."

"Well, think about it." She stood, threw her napkin on her seat, and steamed toward the rest room. Jack watched her go, then asked the waiter to bring him a beer. He had not seen her this way in a long time.

Every other week Jack had dinner with his ex. 8:30 P.M., Moctezuma's Mexican Restaurant, almost a tradition by now. It had started the summer before with a telephone call from a shrink.

Dr. Hillman Roberts had reached Jack at his apartment one afternoon. "I left several messages on your answering machine," he said.

"I got 'em." Jack sat on the couch, watching the Rangers lose on TV while he nursed a foul mood that had lasted most of a year. He considered himself a recovering no-account who had fallen off the wagon.

"I apologize for disturbing you at home, but I have a problem to discuss."

The Rangers brought in another pitcher. Jack thought about the psychiatrist he had used for murder trials when he worked for the district attorney's office. Everybody called the man Doctor Doom: a smooth older gentleman able to take the stand day after day, case after case, and say he had carefully examined all the evidence, and the defendant was a violent sociopath who should be deep-fried. Then Doctor Doom would go back to his suite and wait for his check.

"What kind of problem?" Jack asked the doctor on the phone.

"Frankly, it's about you. And it's about Kathy Brooks."

"You're giving me her last name," Jack said, "in case I have trouble remembering someone I used to be married to."

"I've been seeing her on a regular basis. And I—"

"Seeing?"

"As a patient."

"Hey, you never know."

"This is a professional call."

"Does that mean I have to pay you?"

The doctor cleared his throat. "I'm beginning to understand what Kathy meant about you."

Jack was about to ask, The hell does that mean? But the doctor interrupted with, "Let's try this later. Goodbye."

He listened to the click of the hang-up, then the racing ambulance sound of a phone off the hook, and finally the dead line. Jack held the receiver to his ear, thinking the whole world was at the other end, but first you had to punch a few numbers and say, Hello, let's talk.

The Rangers lost, and Jack stayed on the couch while a rerun of *CHiPs* came on. Ponch was bummed about girl problems but felt better when he caught a hit-and-run driver.

After they booked the hit-and-runner, Jack turned the TV off. He picked up the phone, called information, and reached Dr. Hillman Roberts at home.

A week later he and Kathy were sitting together in the doctor's office, side by side in expensive-looking chairs. Hillman Roberts had a gray combover and one bad eye that drifted to the left. He said to Jack, "What we're going to do is let Kathy drop some burdens she's been carrying."

Which she did, all over Jack. He couldn't say he didn't deserve it. "You threw me out with the trash," she said to him more than once.

Jack sat and listened, squirming but not arguing, while Kathy gave her history of their marriage. "How many others," she asked him, "did you screw around with before you finally got caught?"

Before he could say something clever, like, Give me

time to count that far, she jumped from her chair, straddled his legs, and began to strike his shoulders and chest
with her tiny fists. Jack didn't move, letting the blows rain
on him, while Kathy cried and demanded, "How many?
How many?"

When the hour was done Dr. Hillman Roberts said,
"We have much exploring to do."

The next week's session was tamer, with no fists
headed Jack's way. But the theme was the same—how one
jerk destroyed a marriage. "The thing about you?" Kathy
said at one point. "You don't care about anybody. That's
what your problem is."

Kathy stared at him, waiting for an answer. The doctor
raised expectant eyebrows. Jack gazed out the window,
then said, "Whether it's a problem or not, I can't say."

It went on for four or five weeks. While Kathy and
Jack picked each other's scabs, the doctor's job was to nod
and say, "Go with that."

Finally Jack got Kathy on the phone one day. "You're
paying this half-blind quack one-twenty-five an hour," he
said, "and all you're doing is talking to me. Let's have dinner and you can do that for free."

Now Kathy returned from the Moctezuma's rest room,
more composed, the fire in her eyes having burned down
to the coals she would roast Jack on. "All right, let's hear
it," she said as she took her chair. "Tell me what you did to
Tony."

"You know, Kathy, I never figured you for the type to
date a wormy little guy with a pigtail."

"It's a ponytail."

"Whatever."

42

"Tell me," she said again. "I want to hear it all. Like what you did that got you thrown in jail."

Jack cleared his throat. "I was having a drink with a friend from the attorney general's office, Eddie Wells. Remember him? We're over at the Tradewinds talking some business."

"You're having a drink."

"We were talking business."

"Your stories never start out with, I was talking to my minister. Or, I was at the art museum. You're always in a bar, or with some criminal."

"Eddie and I finish our business and he leaves. I down my last, I'm picking up my change, I'm ready to go, I'm off the goddamn barstool, right? When I hear some jerk behind me say, 'Tony Angel Productions, study in failure, take one.'"

"He called you that?" Kathy sipped some water to hide a smile.

"Like this clown is some big success. What the hell's he got to be all pumped up about? Some show on Hooterville TV?"

"It's on Farmers Branch Telecable," Kathy said. "I've seen it and it's very good."

"So I turn around," Jack said, "and it's your scrawny little boyfriend, Cecil B. De-fuckhead of Farmers Branch, holding a TV camera, pointed at me. He's wearing his leather pants and his shirt open down to here and enough rings that you'd think he robbed Sammy Davis Jr.'s grave. And next to him, it gets even better. There's a guy with a shaved head and combat boots, and he's sticking a boom mike my way."

"That was Mitch. He's Tony's assistant."

"He looks like something from the Appalachian branch of the Hitler Youth, you ask me."

"They're video artists, okay?"

"Yeah, well, this time they were just a couple of ass-holes blocking the cigarette machine. Then one of them turns on the camera light. Ever see that done in a place like the Tradewinds? I thought Kelton was gonna come out from behind the bar and knock the shit out of both of them."

"Tony," Kathy announced, leaning forward, "has a federal grant, Jack. To make videos."

"So Kelton says ... " Jack stopped and grinned. "I mean he's what, seventy years old and ninety-five pounds?"

"How should I know?"

"Kelton yells at them, 'You two fruits kill the light.' Just like that. And they did, they turned it off and sat down at a table. He's a very obedient little boy, that friend of yours."

Kathy took this in and said, "The sex with Tony is great."

"You were waiting to land that one, weren't you?"

"Why should you care, Jack? Why should it bother you?" Jack didn't have an answer. Kathy said, "You still haven't explained what happened. I mean, you did wind up getting arrested."

"Ask your boyfriend. He was there."

"He won't talk about it. He won't even let me see him since it happened."

"He's in seclusion now?" Jack laughed. "Tell me this.

What the hell kind of name is Tony Angel?"

Kathy nailed Jack with her eyes. "His name is Anthony D'Angelo. What did you do to him?"

First of all, Jack said, he couldn't leave the Tradewinds once the two vi-dey-o arteests had arrived. "You understand that, don't you?" he asked.

"Not really."

Because, Jack explained, it would look as if he were running away. So he had another drink, his back to them, biding his time, with Tony talking loud enough to be heard over the jukebox.

Jack had listened to Tony saying: Mitch, you should catch the stories Kathy tells me about this piece of work here. You should hear what he did. And look at him now, Mitch, sitting on that stool, look at the cheap crap he wears. Saying, Mitch, if I ended up like that I'd jump off a frigging cliff. Seriously, I would, Mitch.

"What kind of stories," Jack asked Kathy, "have you been telling him about me?"

"True ones."

Tony's monologue went on and on. Mitch, Tony said, the man has the morals of a snake, the way I heard it. For the way he treated Kathy, Tony said, they oughta lock him up.

After a couple of minutes of this Jack left half his drink and placed three singles on the bar. He turned toward the two. The one with the shaved head was working on his sound equipment. Tony faced away from Jack, still talking. Saying, Mitch, I make love to Kathy three times a night, she tells me she never had it so good. We're doing it, she shouts my name so loud that the walls shake.

Tony sat at one of the wicker chairs Kelton had introduced into the Tradewinds a while back. That and a couple of plastic palm trees were supposed to make the place
look like a beach resort instead of a dump on Henderson
Avenue.

The back of the chair fanned out large and thronelike.
It had black wicker trim and diamond-shaped holes.
Tony's ponytail protruded through one of the holes. Jack
motioned Kelton over.

Tony kept talking as Jack approached. Saying, I told
Kathy, Don't even talk to him anymore, don't waste your
time on a frigging loser.

Jack stood behind Tony's chair, holding a pair of scissors that Kelton had given him. One quick snip and the
ponytail was in Jack's hand. Tony never felt it. Jack tossed
the hair onto the table.

"It landed in his basket of popcorn," Jack told Kathy.
"You should have heard him scream."

On Friday morning Jack had breakfast at Greenie's 24-HR Coffee Shop on East Grand, then went upstairs to work. For six months he had rented Suite Number Two in Greenie's Office Building: one room, clean and carpeted, with a desk, a couch, and a couple of chairs. He could look out his window and see the blinking neon frog on the Greenie's sign.

Jack spent about two hours on the computer and the phone, trying to find pieces of the puzzle. As the licensee of an establishment serving alcohol, Rex Echols had a paper trail. He was forty-one, with a mortgage on his two houses, a lien on his commercial building, and payments to make on a Lincoln Town Car. His credit card balances were slopping over the rim. Last year the city had had to file on him before he paid his back property taxes.

There wasn't much on the late Mingo Gideon. He had owned a 1987 Oldsmobile, and his driver's license listed his address as an apartment complex in far North Dallas. He had stood six-two, weighed 195, and had brown hair and brown eyes.

Mingo possessed no taxable property other than the car and carried no credit cards that Jack could find. A check of court records turned up a couple of indictments, but no convictions, for gambling.

Jack called a Dallas police sergeant in Auto Theft who used to work Vice. The sergeant thought he remembered Mingo as a poker player and gave Jack a couple of names. One of them, Jerry Simpson, answered when Jack phoned. "Yeah, I'll talk to you," he said. "If you come out now, before Mrs. Simpson gets back." He gave Jack an address on Garland Road, out past Buckner Boulevard.

Simpson's Vacuum Cleaner Sales and Service sat at the center of a shabby, block-long retail strip. Some upright carpet sweepers were displayed in Simpson's window, along with a couple of faded FINAL CLOSEOUT banners. Jack walked into the narrow, cluttered shop and found Jerry Simpson behind the cash register. He was shuffling cards on a Formica counter that had been worn through to its backing.

"I heard about poor old Mingo," Jerry said.

"Friend of yours?"

"Mingo? Shit. You find somebody says he was a friend of Mingo's, you let me know. That's a job'll take a detective for sure."

Jerry was a small man who smoked Salems. For a time, he said, he had made his living at poker, playing cards while Mrs. Simpson ran the store. He had stuck to Texas and Louisiana, mostly, but hit Vegas a few times a year. "Things change, you know. Three months ago I gave it all up. Had to make a choice—cards or Mrs. Simpson."

"You know Mingo pretty well?"

"We made the same circuit. Not a bad player, but a sour sonofabitch, tell you that. We called him Mingo No-Bird. See, he was missing the middle finger of his right hand. So he couldn't, you know, give anybody the F-U sign from that side."

Simpson took the deck of cards and began to shuffle again. "I remember somebody asked him once, Mingo, what the hell happened to your finger? Just to see if we could get a few words out of him. And Mingo, he actually starts talking, how he was in the Special Forces and he got it shot off trying to free a buddy from a jungle prison."

Jack looked at the little man surrounded by Hoover spare parts and vacuum cleaner bags. "You believe any of it?"

"Not unless it was a scotch and water they was holding prisoner." Jerry Simpson had a soundless laugh full of yellow teeth.

Jack asked a few more questions, and got a few more answers that weren't much good. Simpson didn't know of any family Mingo might have had, or traveling companions. He could give Jack the names and numbers of some other players, he said, but it wouldn't help. "I guarantee you not a one of 'em knows much of Mingo. Or wanted to."

"He must have hung with somebody. What about a girlfriend?"

"Tell me this. Mingo have a big crowd at his graveside service?" Jerry Simpson parked his cigarette on the lip of an empty chicken pot pie tray and dealt two hands of cards.

"I don't think he even had a funeral."

"There you go."

"Come on, he wasn't a hermit."

"Might as well have been." Simpson pointed to the cards. Jack picked up his hand. He had three nines. "What did he do when he wasn't playing cards?"

"A guy plays cards for a living, that's what he does. When the game's over, he goes back to his motel and sleeps a little, then he moves on to the next game." Simpson swept Jack's discards to the side and dealt him two more. "All I can say is, whenever there was a big game, here come Mingo with a big roll of bills and a face like his stomach hurts."

Jack had picked up two sixes. "He carried a lot of money?"

"Every player packs a bankroll. It's a tool of the trade. But Mingo had a tough time putting his fingers around his wad, it was that huge. His way of saying, you know, Hey, try and take it." Simpson studied his cards and blew a cloud of smoke at the ceiling. "Now if I was a betting man, I'd bet you have a full house."

Jack laid his hand on the counter face up and looked at Simpson's grin. It turned into a big yellow smile when Simpson spread his own cards for Jack to see. Four kings.

"When they pulled his body from the lake," Jack said, "he only had about a hundred bucks on him."

Simpson's eyes narrowed. "No way in the world."

Jack flipped to a page in his notebook. "One hundred and three dollars."

"Lemme tell you what." Simpson pointed with his cigarette. "If I was looking at this instead of you? And somebody tried to tell me Mingo Gideon went anywhere but the bathtub with just pocket change on him? I'd say, Boys, Jerry Simpson ain't that dumb. I'd tell 'em, Hey, when Jerry Simpson gets fed a line of bull like that, Jerry Simpson starts to—uh-oh."

Simpson swept the cards into a stack and dropped them into their box. He mashed the cigarette out and stashed the chicken pot pie tray, the pack of Salems, and the cards in a drawer beneath the cash register. As he waved his hand to clear the smoke he looked toward the front window.

Jack followed his gaze to the parking lot, where a large, scowling woman was getting out of her car. "It's Mrs. Simpson," Jerry Simpson explained.

Preston Road ran straight and smooth out of North Dallas, along the route of an old frontier trail. Comanches had hunted buffalo here. Settlers had died trying to claw a living from the black dirt. Jack thought about this as he waited in the drive-thru lane at I Can't Believe It's Yogurt. He vaguely recalled it from the Texas history he had taken in high school.

Coach Butch Wooster taught Jack's class. Butch Wooster liked to explain everything by diagramming football plays on the blackboard. The defenders at the Alamo, the coach liked to say, didn't have enough blocking up front.

Once, when Coach Wooster was telling how Tom Landry had done more for Texas than Sam Houston, a student raised her hand. Peggy Hart, a cute girl with a nice body but try getting your hands under that dress, was the story on her. Now she asked the coach, out of the blue, "What about fate?"

The coach froze for a moment, stunned, the way the

slaughterhouse hog must look the split second after the sledgehammer drops. Then he came to life with, "Huh-uh, no ma'am." He whirled and began to draw X's and O's on the blackboard. "Halfback has the ball. Line's cleared a hole for him up the middle. Here he comes." A chalk vector showed the halfback's path.

"You're the linebacker," the coach said, staring down Peggy Hart. "You blow a tackle, don't go blaming fate. That's a fairy excuse. Either you make the play or you don't. No such thing as fate."

Jack Flippo, almost twenty years out of high school, had forgotten just about everything he had learned there. Coach Butch Wooster on fate he remembered.

Now, driving north on Preston through the march of the suburbs across the prairie, Jack saw himself as a blackboard X, trying to locate the O that was Mingo Gideon's apartment. He had the address from Mingo's license. A few glimpses at the map, a right at the light, then a left, and he found it.

Creekside Village North was like hundreds of other apartment complexes in and around Dallas. Brick over particleboard, two stories, fake mansard roof with cedar shingles. Thrown up in a hurry back when the money was flowing. The slums of the twenty-first century.

Jack checked with the Creekside Village North office to get Mingo's apartment number, see if he had a roommate.

"Mingo Gideon," repeated the office manager, a thin woman with a landlord's stare. She studied his file. "Moved out end of November. No goodbye and no forwarding address."

Next stop on the day's tour of homes was that of the

witness Bobby Slater. Jack couldn't run the usual computer traps because he didn't have the full name or date of birth. But there was a Bobby Slater in the Dallas phone book. Jack drove to a clapboard house on McGraw Street, nearly to Mesquite.

It was the kind of neighborhood where the driveways filled with pickup trucks after quitting time. Bobby Slater's lawn was unmown brown. A yellow, rolled-up newspaper lay in it. The curtains in the front window were closed. Jack walked to the porch and saw old circulars hanging on the doorknob.

He rang the bell twice and knocked three times. Envelopes and catalogs filled the mailbox hanging next to the door. Jack pulled a postcard from it and saw a picture of sunset at Galveston. "Why am I at the beach in December in the rain?" said neat handwriting in green ink. "And where are you? Been trying to call. Love, Sally."

Jack was about to inspect the rest of the mail when he heard a voice say, "Bobby ain't here." He turned to see a man—skinny, acne scars, late twenties, dirty jumpsuit—in the yard next door. The man had dark, greasy hair and small, close-together eyes that made Jack think of first cousins in love. With a smile Jack came off the porch and offered his business card. He said he wanted to talk to Bobby for an insurance matter. "Whud I just tell you?" the man said.

Jack got him to loosen up enough to say that he was the owner of the house where Bobby lived, that he hadn't seen him for a while, that it was cold out here and he didn't feel like answering any more questions.

"Does he have any friends or family that you know of?" Jack asked.

"I don't stick my nose in my tenants' stuff." The man walked past Jack and up the steps to Bobby's porch.

"Where does he work?" Jack said.

"Ask Bobby." The man gathered the mail from the box.

Jack watched him come back down the steps. "If you see Bobby," Jack said, "you ask him to give me a call?"

"Screw that." The man walked to his own yard and into his house without looking back. Jack bent to pick up the newspaper in Bobby's brown grass and pulled it from its muddy plastic bag. The front page was damp. It was dated November 30, the same day that Mingo No-Bird went in the lake.

9 Five or six cars were in the parking lot of the Melon Patch Ranch when Jack pulled in. It was just after three in the afternoon. He walked through the front entrance, where a large, bored doorkeeper gave him the up-and-down, then waved him through.

Once his eyes adjusted to the dark, Jack counted fewer than a dozen people at the tables. A waitress in a skimpy top and see-through pants moved among them. The place smelled of smoke and spilled beer.

Jack sat at the bar. "What can I get you?" asked the bartender, a woman who didn't look as if she belonged there. She was pretty and tall, but thin, in her twenties, and fully dressed. Jack said he wanted to see the owner. She asked his name, nodded, and picked up the phone next to the cash register.

Within a minute a short, round man took the stool next to Jack. "Well, your day just got better," he said and stuck out his hand. "I'm Rex Echols."

Rex wore a straw cowboy hat and dark glasses, and had a couple of turquoise rings on stubby fingers. His brown beard was cut close over fat cheeks, and he talked in a twang routed through his nose. He looked like a man who never pushed back if a bite remained on the plate. Rex pointed his hat toward a door at the rear of the room. "Less go on back to the office and talk."

His office had a low ceiling, fluorescent lights, and no windows. Country-and-western album covers from the old days hung on the walls. Willie Nelson's *Wishing You a Merry Christmas. Golden Favorites* by Ernest Tubb and the Texas Troubadors. Kitty Wells singing *Dust on the Bible.* On a file cabinet was a framed sampler that read, "Yes, I DO Know Shit."

"Take a load off," Rex said. Jack settled onto a tired blue couch and Rex took his seat behind his desk, across the room. An expanse of carpet stretched between them, harvest gold but not this year's crop. "How about a drink?" Rex asked.

"Coffee would be nice."

"There's a funny story behind that."

Jack waited. Rex said, "Old boy who comes in here ever afternoon about—" He checked his watch. "Well, any minute now. Loves to eyeball the girls, but all he drinks is coffee. Says he's Church of Christ so he don't touch the liquor. Now how I'm supposed to run a club sellin' fifty-cent cups of coffee is way beyond me. But we brew him a pot. See it's ready."

Rex picked up the phone, spoke for a few seconds, and turned to Jack again. "Well, now. I been expectin' you."

"The word's gotten around, I guess."

"Small town like Baggett . . . " Rex shrugged. "Hard to keep a secret, even for the inshurnce company."

Jack rose, put a business card on the desk, and returned to the couch. "I'm working for Continental Centurion. It's a routine investigation."

"Not one a my girls has a cesarean."

Jack looked at Rex Echols' dark glasses.

"A lot of your no-cover clubs, you'll see some girls with scars. Not here."

"Standards," Jack said.

"Izzackly." Rex stood in a hurry. "Lemme show you what I mean." He went to the door and bellowed down the hallway, "April! Right now, April!" As he walked back behind his desk Rex said, "Wait'll you see this, friend. Hold on tight to your eyeballs, 'cause they might pop right outta your head."

Jack decided to keep his hands where they were, take his chances. "I need to ask you a few questions about Mingo Gideon's death."

Rex held up one finger, nodded, and smiled. "We call her April Showers. And yes, I come up with that name."

The bass notes from the showroom speakers rattled the walls. Rex parked his lizardskin boots on his desk and picked up an acoustic guitar. "Long as we got to wait a bit, here's a little song I'm workin' on." He strummed a few chords and sang in a low warble:

> Let's go for a spin in my Coupe De Ville,
> 'Cause babe, I'm a fellow with couth to kill.

Rex stopped when a woman walked in. "May I present to you," he said, "Miss April Showers."

April wore a black Harley-Davidson T-shirt that hung

to mid-thigh. She was blonde, with a face that was about to make the turn from girlish to hard case. Her fingernails were painted purple, and Jack thought at first she had slammed a car door on her hand.

"What is it, Rex? I was on the commode, okay?"

Rex said, "Show Mr. Flippo what you got."

She looked at Jack, then back at Rex. "Show him what?"

"Show him," Rex said, "those factory-installed high-beams."

April Showers shrugged, turned toward Jack, and pulled her T-shirt up to her shoulders. She was naked beneath the shirt. "Well?" Rex said. April Showers seemed to be waiting for an answer, too.

"You're right," Jack said. "No scar. And the floral display is nice."

"Thank you, April." Rex clapped four times. "Top quality, as always. You're the cream in my coffee. And other places."

While Rex laughed out loud, April rolled her eyes, dropped her shirt, and left the room. "The reason I call her April Showers," Rex said when he recovered from his own hilarity, "is I got plans someday to start up a topless club. And when that happens, what I wanna do is build a shower stall on the stage. A shower that works, I'm talkin' about. Glass walls, brass fixtures. Hot, steamy water. Look here."

He took a spiral notebook from a shelf, flipped to a middle page, and held it so Jack could see a pencil sketch. "Bottom line is, April takes a bath onstage," Rex said. "Soaps herself up real nice, lots of steam, good music. They'll be lined up around the block to see that."

Jack was about to tell him, Let's talk about Mingo Gideon, when Rex said, "So that's just one a the reasons Mingo's death was such a tragedy. Rest his poor soul. I mean, that shower thing? Mingo's idea, every bit of it."

"A visionary," Jack said.

"Damn straight."

Rex took the next three or four minutes to deliver a eulogy. Mingo Gideon, true friend, gentleman, generous business partner, one heck of a poker player. "He was a Vietnam vet, you know."

"I heard that's what he told people."

"Hey, the man got the Purple Heart. Lost a damn finger over there."

Jack nodded, doing the math, thinking that Mingo was thirty-three when he died and the country got out of Vietnam in the early seventies. "A twelve-year-old Purple Heart winner," Jack said. "I missed that story."

Rex wasn't listening. "I told him that night, 'Mingo, old buddy, don't go out in that damn boat.' Did I say 'told?' Shit, I begged him, 'Mingo, don't do it.' But he says, 'I feel like a ride.' Middle of the night, you've put away some beers, you don't jump in a boat and take out acrosst a dark lake. You just don't—here she is with that coffee."

The bartender Jack had spoken to came in with a plain white mug and handed it to Jack. She wore black jeans and a loose, long-sleeved black shirt buttoned to the top, with no jewelry or makeup that Jack could see. Her hair was dark and cut even with her chin, and her skin was the color of someone who stayed inside all day.

Jack took the coffee from her and got a tight smile with

it. Rex said, "Good job, Miss Sally." As she turned and walked out Jack remembered the postcard he had pulled from Bobby Slater's mailbox. From Galveston, signed in green ink, "Love, Sally."

"I begged him, 'Mingo, don't go out in that boat.' But he didn't listen." Rex sank into his chair, took off his hat, and ran a hand through a failing batch of hair. "So I lost a good friend and investor. Now, before you ask do I know what happened, I don't. All I can tell you is, he took off in the boat and come back a dead man."

"What were you doing at the lake that night?"

"We was fishin' and there was an accident and I lost my capital source. Where do you think all those poker winnins went? Right into this bidness."

"Who goes fishing," Jack asked, "in the middle of a cold night?"

Rex wiped two fingers along his desktop and checked for dust. "All right, Mr. Continental Centurion, I guess that's a fair question." He took off his glasses and rubbed small, dark eyes that looked like two black olives floating in milk.

"When Mingo died, it tore me up," he said. "I don't mind tellin' you that Rex Echols broke down and cried. Them tears fell like rain."

He put the glasses back on. "But to answer your question, we wasn't really fishin'. We wanted to drink some beer, that's all. No law against that, last time I looked."

"You had the cremation done right away."

"Family wishes. I called Mingo's mama and she said, 'Rex, we're all just brokenhearted here, we'd be mighty grateful if you'd handle it for us.' The least I could do."

"Called her where?"

"Somewhere up in Arkansas, I forget the town." He opened his lap drawer and stared inside. "You know, I don't think I even saved the number."

"And the family didn't want to come to the funeral?"

"Look." Rex shook his head. "These people are just a buncha poor Arkies that don't got a pot to piss in. They're old and they're sick and they're not the kinda people that goes out and jumps on a jet plane."

April Showers was back in the room, unhappy. "There's four lightbulbs burned out around the makeup mirror," she said.

Rex looked at Jack. "Are we about finished here?"

"A couple more questions."

"Plus," April said, "there's only like two clean towels in the supply cabinet and the bathroom's out of soap."

"People think," Rex said to Jack, "that when you run a club you don't do nothin' but look at nice tits all day." April Showers turned and left. Rex said, "The people who think this is fun? I wish they could be here when I got about three girls all with their periods at the same time."

"Bobby Slater," Jack said.

"Bobby? Shit." Rex gave him something close to a laugh. "Don't get me started on Bobby." He stuck one hand in a jeans pocket, fished around the jingling change, and came back out with a nail clipper. Jack watched while Rex trimmed one fingernail. "What else?" Rex said when he finished.

"The sheriff said Bobby Slater was there that night. With you and Mingo."

Rex scratched behind one ear. "Oh, yeah, he was there

all right. Bobby worked for me around this place. All this noise about lightbulbs and towels? Bobby's job was to handle that stuff, keep the girls happy. We brought him along that night to fetch beer and sandwiches, that's all."

Jack said he wondered when Bobby would show up for work.

"Bobby quit." Rex stood. He was one of those people who looked shorter when he left a chair. "The day after we got back from the lake, he calls in and leaves me a message that he don't work here no more. Do me a favor. When you talk to Bobby? Tell him Rex Echols don't rehire people that quits without notice. Tell him he'll never work at the Melon Patch again . . . Hey, I'd love to talk some more." Rex came around his desk with his hand extended. "But I got a bidness to run. Some other time, maybe."

They shook hands. "How about tomorrow?" Jack asked.

Rex held the handshake. "I can't believe one inshurnce company has so many questions. Let me ask you one. Five hunnerd thousand dollars can't be that much to a big old corporation. So what's all the excitement about?"

Jack took back his hand. "It's not small change."

"I mean, you're runnin' around like Rex Echols is on some scam." He said it with a smile.

Jack smiled back. "Just doing what I was hired to do."

"Suppose I was to hire you? You know what I'm talkin' about? We could make an arrangement."

Jack looked around at the record album covers. He felt Buck Owens staring at him.

"Don't be hasty," Rex said. "Think it over."

April Showers was in the office again, this time

dressed in a couple of ounces of spangled fabric, saying, "I've had it with this place."

"Be right with you, baby." Rex reached up and slapped Jack's shoulder. "Good to see you. Come on by anytime. Like I said, think about it, you workin' for me. We could talk some more."

Jack gathered his papers and his coffee cup. "You mind if I sit at the bar for a few minutes?" He raised his mug. "Maybe have another cup?"

Rex extended an arm toward the door. "Hey, you don't have to hang back. Get yourself a seat at a prime table."

"That's okay."

"Get down there in the front row. Fantasyland, I call it. Makes you feel like there's lightnin' strikin' your zipper."

"The bar'll be fine."

"We'll talk some more later," Rex said.

Jack walked out of the office, down the hall, into the showroom, and to the bar. The bartender, Sally, was shaking a margarita. Jack sat on the closest stool and leaned her way. "Other than rainy," he asked her, "how was Galveston?"

There was a hitch in her shaking, and she met his eyes before looking away. Her glance had been on him only a second or so. It was long enough for Jack to see plenty.

Sally Danvers could feel the man's stare on her as she poured the drink. She glanced at him again. He didn't look away. After she set the drink at the wait station she turned back to him. "What can I get you?" she said. He didn't answer for a moment.

She had noticed him when he came in, even before he asked to talk to Rex. He wasn't the usual customer, because he didn't just sit and put a brain-dead gaze on the girls. His eyes had been all over the room.

Now he was looking at Sally but not answering when she asked what he wanted. "Something for you?" she said in a tone meant to tell him, in a club like this on Northwest Highway, where guys you wouldn't share a sidewalk with would lean across the bar and suggest that you give them oral sex on the spot, that it would take more than a stare to shake her up. Finally he said, "Galveston in December, at least you don't have to worry about the crowds." Sally studied him for a few seconds, see how he liked being sized up. He was tall and thin with a nice jaw and a big nose. No wedding ring and not bad looking. His blond hair needed styling and his suit could use a press. He would have seemed harmless enough except for the way he inspected her like someone taking inventory.

She folded her arms on the bar. "You trying to start a conversation with this Galveston bit? All right, it's started. Now, what is it?"

"My name is Jack Flippo. I'm an investigator."

Sally kept her arms folded. "Is that your pickup line? You need a new one."

"I'd like to talk to you when you get off. It's about a friend of yours."

"Maybe I don't have any friends," she said.

"I'm starting to see why." He smiled.

The phone beside the cash register buzzed. Sally turned her back on Jack Flippo the investigator. "Listen here," Rex Echols said when she answered, "tell that dude at the bar you'll be right back. Then come see me."

"I seen him talking to you. What's he want to know?" Rex sat behind his desk and cracked his knuckles one by one.

"So far, nothing," Sally answered from the doorway. "He just said he wants to talk to me after work."

"These damn inshurnce companies." Rex rubbed the back of his neck. "I got a claim and they don't want to pay. They took my premiums, no problem there. Ever time I'm a week late with the check they let me hear about it. But when it's time for them to pay me, they send some squirrel in a suit around to ask questions. Burns me the hell up."

Sally stepped away, figuring Rex could rant and rave

alone. "Miss Sally," he called, the tone friendly all of a sudden. She came back to the door. "How'd you like," he said, "to make an extra hunnerd bucks today? And get off early?"

"For what?"

Rex took his wallet from his pocket and opened it. "All you got to do—that's twenty, forty, sixty, eighty, and ten and ten—is go have a talk with that snoop, find out what he wants to know, and report back to me. Here you go, babe."

Sally looked at the hand with the money. Rex waved the bills and said, "Easy money, to my way of thinking."

For an instant she saw herself back on the beach in Galveston. There had been a raw wind off the Gulf, with no sun and a low, heavy sky. Sally had waded into the cold surf, her jeans soaked past the knees. She stood shivering and holding herself, looking out to the far edge of the water. Gray foamy waves tumbled past her and washed back out. The undertow tugged at her feet, trying to drag her out, too. There had been a time when she would have let it.

She stored the thought away, not sure why it had popped up. The blond guy looked like someone she could talk with if she had to. "All right," she said as Rex handed the money to her. "Why not?"

The man was still at the bar. So was a waitress with two drink orders. Sally filled them, then turned to her audience of one. "Maybe I was a little rude before."

"It's forgotten."

"What is it you want?"

"I'd like to talk to you about someone you know.

Maybe when you get off we could . . . "

"Four-thirty?"

"Sure."

Sally took a pen from a cup next to the cash register and handed it to Jack along with an open Melon Patch matchbook. "Write down where you want to meet."

He wrote *The Tradewinds, on Henderson N. of Ross.* Sally looked at the matchbook. "Never heard of it."

"It's on Henderson, north of Ross."

"I can read." She slipped the matchbook in her pants pocket.

"That was easy."

"Yeah, it was," she said, turning away. "Be on time."

Mitch walked into the studio, which was what Tony Angel called the spare bedroom in his condo. He studied Tony for a few seconds and said, "For real, man, it don't look too bad. I mean, if you think about what happened."

Tony raised his hand for silence the way Jack Lord did on *Hawaii Five-O* reruns. "It looks like shit, Mitch. Don't tell me it doesn't. I got eyes, I checked the mirror. It looks like I got jumped by a chimp with some clippers."

Mitch shrugged and dropped into a chair. "Just trying to beam you up."

Tony moved before a mirror and ran shaky, delicate fingers over the place where his ponytail had been. "The guy committed hair rape, all right?"

Mitch squeezed a pimple next to his nose ring. "You got hairjacked." He snorted a few laughs and rubbed his shaved scalp. "I guess I'm like immune to it."

"He's a lucky frigging guy, that guy. You know what I'm saying, Mitch? He's lucky I'm Aquarius, for one. He's lucky I'm an artist and not the muscle I could be. Guys I grew up with in Jersey? You think they wouldna reached down his throat, grabbed onto his prostrate gland, and turned him inside out like a fucking dirty sock?"

Mitch wiped his nose on the back of his hand. "You hungry, man? Want to grab some lunch?"

"Hey, I worked Atlantic City for two years. Two years, Mitch, who do you think did all the promotional videos for Caesar's? Tony Angel Productions, that's who. You're in your room at Caesar's, you turn on the house channel, whose work did you see? That's right, Tony Angel's."

"'Cause I was thinking maybe we could grab a burger."

"You know what Hackett told me? Right in his dressing room, he's standing there, he's shaking my hand. Buddy Hackett, Mitch. He says, Tony, there's nobody better with a camera. He says, Tony, you're an artist. Top that. Straight from the mouth of one of the greats, nobody better than yours truly ... So if I'm playing in the big leagues at Caesar's, Mitch, if I'm running with major packs, you think I don't know what happens to guys like this jerkoff, they fuck with the wrong people? I'll tell you what happens. They end up in three suitcases at the bottom of the Intracoastal. So he's a lucky frigging guy ... Jesus, look at that garbage she's pushing."

Tony stared at a woman selling glass statuettes of songbirds on TV. Mitch took a disposable lighter from the pocket of his jeans and began to flick it on and off, gazing at the flame and then at the empty space where the flame had been and then at the flame again. "Tony, man, you feel like hitting the clubs tonight?"

"Right, Mitch, and just what am I supposed to do about this?" Tony's hand floated over the back of his head.

Mitch flicked his lighter on and off. "I guess, like wear a hat?"

"Oh, that's cute. Thank you so much. Maybe if some wacko in a hockey mask slices off both my arms you'll roll my sleeves up for me, too."

Mitch thought about it for a while. "Hey, Tony, if that really happened? You could be like a master criminal and never get caught. No fingerprints."

Tony didn't respond. They sat in front of the shopping channel for a good thirty minutes, watching pitches for tennis bracelets, chiffon party dresses, and Annette Funicello teddy bears. Tony barely moved, except to stroke the back of his head. Mitch played with his lighter. Thinking it was just like the old days back at the Psychiatric Center, the two of them hanging around the dayroom and staring at the tube, except Mitch wasn't allowed to have his lighter back then.

In the middle of an offer for cutlery Tony said, "That's it, I got it, I know what I want."

Mitch looked up. "Knives, man?"

Tony stood. "What's that song by that band you like, that Donna Reed Nation? You know, *DA-duh, duh-duh-duh-duh-DA-duh.*"

Mitch sat up. "Yeah, yeah . . . really heavy bass line and then the vocals come in, boom, you're like falling into one of those things an elevator moves up and down in." He thought for a moment, then snapped his fingers once and pointed at Tony. "True Love Canal."

"That's the track I'm using."

71

"Outstanding cut, excellent idea," Mitch said, putting down his lighter and drumming his knees. "Using for what?"

"I'm working over our video project. I'm tossing out what we got and I'm starting over. We're gonna shoot the whole thing in black and white, and we're gonna put an attitude on it like you wouldn't believe. You understand what I'm saying?"

"That's a tough question, man."

"Here's what I want. You listening to me? I want Eyewitness News married to a bank surveillance camera, but having a hump with *Funniest Home Videos*. Focus comes in and out. Light goes over and under. Huh? Huh?"

"Cool."

"You watch TV now, Mitch, what do you see? You see frigging amateurs all over the place. You got tape of firemen pulling a kid outta a frozen lake. Change the channel, you got fat ladies with their pants falling down."

"I love that show."

"Check the other side of it, Mitch. Cameras spying on you everywhere you go. You can't walk into a store for a fucking roll of toilet paper without the camera on you. You go to use the toilet paper, they're probably watching you do that, too."

"Crapper-cam," Mitch said.

"So we put all those together, see. We follow our man everywhere he goes. Every move he makes we put on tape." Tony smiled. "Then we get his ex, right? To tell us what an asshole he was, and we intercut our surveillance footage with that. This'll knock people on their ass, they see this, I guarantee you."

"Yeah, but one thing." Mitch flicked the lighter on and off. "I mean, who're you gonna watch?"

"The fuck you been the last hour? I'm talking about the maniac came after me with the scissors."

"That dude? Whoa." Mitch rubbed his head. "Man, in that bar the other night we only got about five seconds of him. How're you gonna—"

The Jack Lord hand went up. "We get a lot more."

Mitch began to play with his lighter again, shaking his head. "I don't know . . . The look on his face when he X'd out your ponytail, he was enjoying it."

"Well, that's the last thing he's gonna enjoy from Tony Angel, I'm seeing to that personally. When I'm finished with this guy, he's gonna beg for mercy. Frigging loser won't know what hit him."

"Tony? What's he gonna cut off of you next time?"

"We put him in jail last time, remember? He's not gonna do anything. He won't touch me."

"Man, the way he was smiling when he had those scissors and your hair . . . "

"Hey, Mitch? Give me some credit here. All right? Trust the artist on this one."

12 Jack drove up Ross Avenue past the used car lots. He turned left at the abandoned Sears, skirted a vacant expanse where a bank building used to be, and parked next to a prosthesis store.

The Tradewinds was across the street.

"There he is!" Kelton bellowed when Jack walked in. "Jack the Barber! C'mere! Lookadis!" He was pointing a knobby finger at something stuck on the wall above the cash register. Jack walked over, squinted, and saw a clump of hair in a clear plastic bag. "It's the guy's tail," Kelton said. "We saved it."

Jack said thanks, asked Kelton to keep it for him, ordered a Shiner dark, and punched up Carl Perkins on the jukebox. He took a table by the front window, in the weak afternoon sun. At just after four-thirty Sally arrived, walking in like someone who knew the place. She glided straight to Jack's table. "What are you drinking?" he asked.

"A beer'll do." Jack signaled to the bar. "You look like a lawyer," she said.

"Used to be."

"I hate lawyers."

"I never heard anyone say that before."

Sally lit a Merit with a match and blew smoke past him. "But now you work for an insurance company?"

"They're a client."

"I hate insurance companies."

A waitress brought two beers. Jack raised his bottle and said, "We're off to a promising start." He watched her smoke her cigarette and saw that she had undone the top two buttons of her black shirt. "Where're you from?" Jack asked.

"Texas City."

"And lived to tell the tale, huh?"

"Oh, you're gonna make fun of Texas City now? Why don't I do it for you. It's ugly and it smells like shit and it's full of oil refineries. How's that? Like Dallas is some kind of paradise."

In the light from the window her eyes were a washed-out blue. She ran a hand through her dark, straight hair. Jack saw no wedding ring.

"What's your last name, Sally?"

She thought about it for a while, then said, "Danvers."

"Miss or Mrs. Danvers?"

Her eyes went over his face. "I'm not married. Is that what you want to know?"

Jack nodded. She said, "I was married, but I'm not anymore."

"I'm sorry."

"Why should you be?" She tapped the ash off her cigarette. "You want to know all about it, I'll tell you. I'll give you the whole sad story. But I don't see what this has to do with anything."

"I'll change the subject."

She stubbed her cigarette in the ashtray. "Good move."

"I'm looking into the drowning death of a man named Mingo Gideon. Also known as Mingo No-Bird. Did you know him?"

Sally shook her head, not interested.

"He was Rex Echols's business partner. Ever heard of him?"

"No, I haven't." Her hands went through her hair again, her eyes on his.

"Bobby Slater," Jack said. Her face clouded over, but she didn't look away. "I would like to talk to your friend Bobby Slater."

"So talk to him. You don't need my permission."

"I might need your help to find him."

Sally studied the ashtray. "Why?" she finally said.

"Because he seems to have disappeared. Bobby was with Rex Echols when Mingo Gideon died." She glanced at him, then looked at the floor. "He hasn't been seen since," Jack said. "Right? Have you seen him?"

Sally didn't answer. "You're his friend?" Jack said. "As a friend, maybe you should be worried that something has happened to him. Maybe you and I could find him, make sure everything's okay."

The bleached blue eyes came back to his. "Your friend Bobby might need your help," Jack said. "He might need my help, too."

Jack thought she was about to open up. He was wrong. "I don't think so," she said, and pushed her chair back. Before he could say anything else she was walking away.

At the Melon Patch Ranch Sally found Rex Echols working the bar. April was waiting tables as a Garth Brooks song played for five or six customers. "Let's hear it," Rex said to Sally. "Which way's that snake crawling?"

"He asked about somebody who drowned. He wanted me to tell him everything I know."

"And what was that?"

"I don't know anything. What could I tell him?"

Rex nodded, took a cocktail toothpick shaped like a tiny sword, and began to work his teeth. "What'd he ask you about Rex Echols?"

"Nothing. His whole deal was this drowning. Who drowned, Rex?"

Rex left the toothpick in his mouth and laid his hands on the bar. Sally watched him clench and unclench his fists. "Damn inshurnce weasels," he said and shook his head. "Okay, Miss Sally, you done good. Enjoy your day off."

Sally started to go, then stopped. "I asked you this the other day, Rex, and you didn't answer. When's Bobby coming back to work?"

Rex stared across the showroom. "He don't work here no more." He turned his face toward Sally. "Why?"

"He quit? When?"

Rex chewed the toothpick. "Hell, I don't remember. Why?"

"Curious, that's all. Where's he working now?"

"Who the hell knows. Hey, I got work to do around

here. I'm busier'n a one-legged man in a butt-kick con-
test."

"Right." Sally nodded.

"Right," Rex said, keeping his eyes on her.

Sally took her purse and left the bar. She crossed the
showroom, zigging and zagging between the tables. At the
door she looked back. Rex was still watching her.

Jack drove from the Tradewinds to his office. He had
been there only ten minutes when Cactus Bloodworth
called from Hawaii, wanting to know how that East Texas
drowning deal was going.

He told Cactus all he knew, and Cactus said, "Sounds
like you're busting the bronc, Jackie."

"Lots of smoke from strange places," Jack said.

"Good deal. How about getting a written report together, drop it by my office tonight. That way my secretary
can fax it up to Continental Centurion tomorrow morning."

"No problem."

"Good deal," Cactus said again. "Well, I gotta roll. The
beach is calling. Do you hear it?"

Jack looked out the window at the gray sky. "Not from
here."

"Talk to you when I get back next week," Cactus said.
"After my Ha-wah-yan wedding. Me and my new bride,
Jack, we'll have you over for a home-cooked dinner to
celebrate . . . What's that, babe? . . . Jack, hold on a sec."
Jack waited while Cactus had a muffled conversation.
"Jack," Cactus said, "my true love Nikki just now
informs me that she doesn't cook. So we'll go out, how's
that?"

"Sounds good."

"We'll go on down to Ruth's Chris, get us some thick steaks, medium rare, and—hold on, Jack." There was more hand-over-the-phone talk on the other end. Then Cactus said, "Well, Jack, Nikki doesn't eat red meat. Got a thing for cows, I guess. All right, maybe we'll do Mexican. You like Mexican, baby? . . . Okay, that's out. Jack, we'll figure out something between now and then."

"Can I ask you a question, Cactus?"

"Fire away."

"How long have you known this woman?"

"Oh, I don't know," Cactus said. "A few weeks. Why?"

It took Jack a couple of hours to put together his file for the insurance company. He reported on the sheriff's records and the death certificate, and summarized his interviews. He noted the lack of autopsy or photographs. He would now spend most of his time, Jack wrote, trying to find the missing witness.

Jack drove to Cactus's office and put the report through the mail slot. He grabbed dinner at a place nearby, reading a magazine while he ate. By ten he was home with a bottle of beer, the sports pages, Roy Orbison on the stereo—maybe not bliss but as close as he had come to it lately.

Just before midnight, as he was about to roll off the couch and go to bed, the phone rang. "This is Sally Danvers," she said, "from this afternoon."

"You just remembered something else about me you don't like?"

"I want to ask you about Bobby."

"Bobby Slater?" Jack said. "Sure."

"What's he done wrong? What kind of trouble is he in?"

"Those are two separate questions."

"You talked like he'd done something against the law. I don't believe that."

"I don't have reason to believe that he's done anything illegal. He's a witness, that's all, and I want to talk to him. Nobody seems to know where he is. If he was someone I cared about, I'd be concerned."

Jack waited. Finally Sally said, "He's my friend."

"I just want to talk to him, nothing else. If you could let me know where—"

"That's the problem."

"You're telling me you can't find him, either."

"Look," she said, and stopped. "I'll give you a place to start. But you have to promise me you're not going to hurt him."

Her words made Jack think of Ken Kinney, a chain-smoking 350-pound lawyer who lived off court appointments. Jack remembered seeing him once in the courthouse hallway, trying to get away from the angry family of a client he'd just screwed. Ken Kinney, with his shirttail coming out and a mess of papers under his arm in a slo-mo cascade toward the floor. Holding a smoldering butt and talking fast and loud. Telling the family, "Sure I gave you my word. But all guarantees are subject to change."

Now the woman said to Jack, "You have to promise me you won't get Bobby in any more trouble."

Any *more* trouble—a loophole. "I promise," Jack said.

She took a deep breath, then said, "Every Monday

afternoon Bobby goes to a house Rex Echols has in East Texas. He's supposed to check on the pool, make sure nobody's broken in, haul off the garbage, things like that."

"Okay."

"Rex has a wife. Barbara. Everyone calls her Baby."

"Baby."

"Every Monday afternoon Baby goes to the house in East Texas, too."

"Uh-huh."

She paused. "Uh-huh," Jack said again.

"Are you thinking this over," Sally asked, "or are you just slow?"

13 "Put this on." Loyce Slapp lifted his shiny black belt and holster from the back of a chair. "Put this on and dance for me some."

"You say somethin'?" April Showers stood in front of a mirror, wearing her Melon Patch thong and working on her hair. "I get around you, Loyce, I feel like I need one of them Mircale-Ears."

"Give me a show." Loyce Slapp, in white jockey shorts he had made his wife iron, approached April from behind. He slipped the belt around her waist and tried to buckle it.

"Give you a what?" She twisted away and bent to pick up her shirt from the floor. "After all that"—she waved toward the twisted sheets of the bed—"you want a show?"

Loyce Slapp sighed, placed his holster back on the chair, and dropped into the bed. The room was costing him $53.95 plus tax. The bourbon had run him ten bucks. He'd used the patrol car for the two-hour drive into Dallas, so he wouldn't have to pay for the gas. Still, figure a meal before he went home to Baggett, and the cost of the evening was coming up on seventy bucks. For that much, he thought, you'd expect a little more than just one roll on the mattress.

"You danced for me last time," he said. "What is it, the gun? I'll take the gun out. Just dance with the leather. And no panties."

April rolled her eyes. "All right. Jesus." She dropped the thong to the carpet. "What do you want me to dance to? You gonna whistle?"

Loyce Slapp reached for the television remote and hopped channels before stopping at MTV. "Don't forget the holster," he said before he raised the volume.

She shook her breasts for him, then turned, bent at the waist, and gave him a view that made Loyce Slapp fall back on his pillow and gasp. No woman in Baggett was made this way.

Loyce wondered how a man could go home after seeing something like that. He thought of his wife, knew exactly how she was dressed right now and what she was doing: She was wearing her huge tent of a pink robe and her baby blue slippers, with her white scarf wrapped around her head. She was tilted back in her groaning Naugahyde recliner. Beside her she had a Diet Sprite and a bag of green-onion-dip-flavored potato chips, or a box of Pop-Tarts if she'd moved on to a second course. On the TV there would be a preacher begging for money. Loyce found her that way every night, even when he came home late. Three or four in the morning, she'd be in the recliner asleep, the TV never off—*and, friends, for a spirit donation of just fifty dollars, we'll send you this personally signed daily prayer and giving guide*—her heavy-framed glasses slightly askew, the snore of chronic sinusitis rising from her.

When April danced close to the bed the sheriff took her hand and pulled her on top of him. "Loyce," she said, "I gotta go."

"Come with me."

April pushed the mute button on the remote. "That's real funny."

Loyce Slapp ran his hands over her. "I'm serious. You and me, together all the time. This once-in-a-while business just won't cut it. After a couple of days I'm dying for you."

April rolled off him and propped herself on her elbow. "Me in some little East Texas hick town? Doing what, hangin' out at the feed store and sweepin' up chicken shit? I grew up in a place like that, buddy. And I ain't about to go back."

"Listen to me," Loyce said.

"If you'd talk a little louder I might be able to."

"We could go somewhere else. A place with a beach, an island. I don't mean just a few days. I mean to live."

"Oh, right."

"Listen, now. I'll say one word to you. Barbados. I saw pictures, what a place that is." He had a brochure with photographs of palm trees and crystal-clear water and handsome couples at an outdoor cafe, drinking piña coladas from coconut shells while happy waiters set the desserts on fire. "You wouldn't believe it, it's so beautiful."

April dropped onto her back and stared at the ceiling. "I got me a 1986 Pontiac Grand Am with transmission trouble, Loyce. You're a county sheriff. Tell me how that gets us to some island."

Loyce had known when he started talking that it would come to this. He wasn't going to say it, but then there was the sight of April bent over, waving her everything at him. It made him want to cry, the beauty of it, the thought of making her his. "We could do it," he said.

"Like how?"

"I have some money coming soon."

April perched herself on her elbow again. "Loyce," she said, smiling and drawing his name out long, stretching it like a piece of gum. He watched her run her fingers over his chest. Purple nails, something else that drove him wild. "Sheriff Loyce," she said, "are you keeping a secret?"

Loyce kissed her breast just below the yellow rose. "You might say it's an inheritance."

"You got a rich uncle?" The nails raked his waistline, headed south.

"Sort of."

"How rich?" she said, getting a grip that made Loyce Slapp's eyes start to roll back into his head.

"Rich enough," he managed to say.

But maybe not, Loyce thought later. After April had gone, he took some motel stationery from the desk in his room and worked calculations with his mechanical pencil. He figured a 6 percent yield on his principal, then an 8 percent, then 10. He called the airlines for fare quotes, and he estimated the cost of renting a two-bedroom condo, ocean view.

Three separate columns of neat figures, tiny numbers all in rows, ran down the paper. Three different totals, all leaving him with the same conclusion: He needed more money.

It was past midnight when he drove the Baggett County patrol car into the parking lot at the Melon Patch Ranch. He walked through the smoky dark past ten or twelve people at the tables and found Rex Echols tending bar.

"Good golly, it's the sheriff." Rex Echols extended a hand to shake. "And it ain't even half-price drink night."

"Let's talk," Loyce Slapp said.

"What I do best, next to singin'."

"In private," he said, and watched Rex Echols blink and try to hang onto his smile.

"What's wrong?"

Loyce Slapp answered with a nod toward the exit at the back of the room. Rex Echols motioned for a waitress to take his place behind the bar. "I'll meet you in your office," Loyce Slapp said.

He went over his figures again while waiting, checking the addition and subtraction. Rex Echols came in singing.

> 'Fore she's through she will marry
> Every Tom, Dick, and Harry,
> And throw in a Billy or two.

Rex could be headed to his own hanging, Loyce Slapp thought, he'd walk to the gallows with a song. The music stopped when Rex hit the chair behind the desk. "So, Sheriff. What's so damn important?"

Loyce Slapp recreased his paper and slipped it back into his shirt pocket. "Those figures we discussed on the settlement? Not enough."

86

The cowboy hat came off, then the dark glasses. Rex Echols rubbed his eyes with both hands. "Sheriff, I been rode hard and put up wet all week. I'm wore out, is what I am. So run that by me again."

"I'm doubling my share."

Rex's hands fell away from his eyes, his jaw dropped, and a barking laugh flew out. He shoved his chair back. For an instant Loyce Slapp thought he would have to fight, and his fingers went under his coat to his gun.

"The fuck're you talkin' about?" Rex said. "Huh? The fuck're you sayin'?"

"I've taken another look at my needs. One hundred thousand won't be enough. Simple as that. I need two-oh-six-five."

"Two?" he blurted. "*Two*?" Loyce watched as Rex's face went red, as he ran a heavy hand over his mouth and cheeks. His stare hit the floor and bounced to the ceiling. He folded his arms tight against himself, as if to keep them from flailing. If Rex let go, Loyce Slapp thought, he'd corkscrew right up through the roof.

Rex kept himself wrapped, and after a while the words came out as if chipped from a rock. "We had an agreement."

"Now we have another one."

"You can't just dance in here—" He stopped to breathe a few times. "Dance in here and hijack my money truck."

"I just did."

"It don't work that way."

"It's working that way now. Think about how it wouldn't work without me."

"Half a million—" Rex broke off, shaking his head. "Half a million dollars in my hands and now it's goin' up in smoke."

"You'll still have three hundred thousand." Loyce was thinking of the sailboat he would buy.

Rex's hands trembled as he put his hat back on. "I shoulda taken a bigger policy. Mingo told me then, told me when I bought it. Said if you're gonna do it, do it big. That's a hell of a note, huh?"

"Next time listen to Mingo."

Rex said, "I mean, givin' you that much off the top. What about Echolsound? I was gonna build a studio . . ." With Loyce thinking, He's going to start pleading now, put a little catch in his voice, turn his eyes all sad. "Givin' you that big a share," Rex said, "I don't see why it should be that way."

Loyce waited until Rex's gaze dragged its way up to meet his. "What choice do you have?" the sheriff asked him.

"What? Do what?"

"I said, what choice do you have?"

Rex looked away and muttered, "This is creamed bull-shit in a china bowl." Loyce rose to leave. Rex said, "That boy from the inshurnce company's been here."

"We expected that."

"Askin' a bunch of questions."

"It's what they do. They ask questions." Loyce placed his hands flat on the desk and looked down at Rex. "What did he get from you?"

Rex backed his chair up and stood. "He didn't get nothin'."

"Well, he's not getting anything in Baggett County, either."

"Well, he drilled a dry hole here."

At his condo in Barbados, Loyce thought, he and April would keep a parrot. Sit out on the patio in their bathing suits at sundown and teach it to talk. He said, "I won't let this be fucked up."

"Hey, the squirrel walked outta the Melon Patch with nothin' to show. If he's gonna find something that hurts"—Rex pointed a finger—"it's gonna be in Baggett."

"You just do your part," Loyce Slapp said, "and I'll do mine."

On Sunday night Jack lay in bed and remembered pictures of the dead ones. He thought about his years in court, with crime scene photographs of victims spread before him on long tables. Pictures of those who were shot, knifed, and beaten. Others had been strangled or run over by cars. Then you had the exotics: poisoned, sawed in half, or hot-wired in the bathtub with a plugged-in hair dryer.

Some had no clothes. The bodies left in the woods had begun to decompose or had been picked apart by animals. Every now and then, though, you got the perfect ones, the wax museum statues. Barely a mark on them, with a press still in their shirts. You would almost think the mortician had been there already. Some of the corpses had their eyes open, others closed. A few had no eyes at all.

He remembered pictures of bodies in ditches, on carpets, inside cars, across beds, in their easy chairs, on golf courses, under floorboards. One especially stood out, a woman almost nineteen who had been murdered and dumped in the Trinity during the spring floods. Only after the water receded did they find her, stuck in the upper branches of a riverside tree as if blown there.

Jack had learned pretty fast that the dead can turn up anywhere.

Late the next morning he left for Baggett. The day was wet and cold, with the radio full of forecasts for freezing rain by nightfall. His plan was to make it home before then.

First stop in town was the office of Justice of the Peace Webb Carroll. Not much had changed. The old poodle lay on the pillow next to the desk, and Webb Carroll played with his toy trains.

"I remember you," he said when Jack walked in. "But refresh my memory, now."

Jack wondered if Webb Carroll had managed to repair his equipment so he could develop the photographs he had taken of Mingo Gideon's body.

"The boy that drowned?" Webb Carroll said. "I give that film to the sheriff not two days ago. Loyce said he'd take care of it."

Jack found Sheriff Loyce Slapp at Dee's Cafe across the street from the courthouse. Dee's had a counter with five round chrome-and-leatherette stools that gave a view of the busy deep-fry vats. Antlers hung on the wall, along with an old Baggett Bandits football schedule and a couple of calendars furnished by makers of diesel-truck parts. Country music played from a radio next to the cash register. A water-stained drop ceiling kept the cigarette smoke haze hanging low.

There were six or seven square tables on the worn green linoleum. The sheriff sat at one near the back, along with one of his deputies and two men in overalls. Loyce Slapp glanced at Jack when he came through the door. Jack nodded at him but got no response, so he stood a few feet from the table and waited for a break in the conversation.

The deputy was talking about someone named Cooter Strickland, whose brother-in-law's brother-in-law had borrowed two dogs without Cooter's permission. "Wanted to take 'em on a hunt," the deputy said.

Cooter had shown his unhappiness by laying a crowbar across his brother-in-law's brother-in-law, breaking one of his arms and two of his ribs. "I ast him," the deputy said, "'Why'd you want to go and hit him with a crowbar?'" He took a sip of coffee. "And Cooter says to me, 'Weren't no gun handy.'"

Everyone laughed but Loyce Slapp. Jack stepped forward and said, "Talk to you, Sheriff?"

Loyce Slapp poured sugar in his coffee cup. "I'm busy right now."

"This will only take a couple of minutes."

"I'm busy."

"With what?" Jack said. "Your coffee break or the adventures of Cooter Strickland?"

Loyce Slapp turned and looked Jack up and down. "When I'm done," he said, almost in a whisper, "I'll let you know."

The two stared at each other until Loyce Slapp broke away to listen to a story about a delivery-truck driver with a hernia. Jack took a stool at the counter while the four at the table talked about trusses, high school basketball, the lumber business, and the weather.

After about ten minutes one of the men in overalls announced, "Time to go to work." The other one joined him. The deputy talked for a minute or two, then left. Jack went to the table, sat in an empty chair, and said, "Ready when you are."

"What is it now?" the sheriff said.

"I'm still working the Mingo Gideon case."

Loyce Slapp stirred his coffee. Jack put his elbows on the table and leaned forward. "I'm told that you now have the film the JP shot of the body. Has it been developed?"

The sheriff put his cup down and fished in his pants pocket, jangling change. "What else can you imagine that I would do with it?"

"I'd like to see the prints."

Loyce Slapp stood and put two nickels on the table next to his cup, stared at the coins, then returned one of them to his pocket. "If you think that'll help," he said and walked out.

Jack followed him from the cafe across the street and into the courthouse. The sheriff went straight to his office, with Jack about ten feet behind him. He waited while Loyce Slapp set his hat on one corner of his almost empty desk, hung his jacket on a coatrack, and smoothed the wrinkles in its sleeves.

"All right," the sheriff said as he settled stiffly into his chair. "You want to see a picture." He opened his lap drawer, checked the label on a manila folder, and placed it on the desk. The label said GIDEON, MINGO. Inside the folder Jack found one black-and-white photo, eight by ten. "Where's the rest?" he said.

"That's the whole show." The sheriff opened a small

pocketknife and began to sharpen a pencil over a waste-basket.

The photo showed the body of a white male, wet, face down, arms folded under him, lying on a rough concrete surface that could have been the boat ramp. He was fully clothed except for one missing shoe. "All right," Jack said, "we've had our fun. I want to see the rest of the shots."

The sheriff paused with his pencil. "I said that's all there is."

Jack tossed the photo on the desk. "The man could have fourteen icepick holes in his forehead, you couldn't tell from this."

Loyce Slapp looked at the picture. "I suppose so."

"And you really don't give a shit, do you?"

"About you? No, I don't." He blew hard on the new pencil point a couple of times, then held it up to admire it. "If the Justice of the Peace," the sheriff said, still looking at the pencil, "decided to take just one picture, then I guess one picture is all you get." He picked up the folder. "You through with this?"

"You keep it," Jack said. "Because one day scientists might discover that losing one shoe could kill someone."

"Don't like the way the job's done," Loyce Slapp said, putting the folder away, "maybe you should move to Baggett and run for justice of the peace."

"Climb every mountain, I always say."

"You could even run for sheriff. But I don't think you'd last too long in this town."

Jack smelled a punch line coming. Something meant to shake him up, heavy with menace but stopping just short of an actionable threat. Guys like this, it was in their blood.

The sheriff didn't disappoint. "I'm not not even sure," he whispered, snapping his knife shut, "you'd last one night."

Jack drove while listening to the afternoon swap meet on KBGT-AM, voice of the greater Baggett County area. Dotty T. had two kitchen chairs to unload. Hank D. was in the market for a couch but nothing that a pet had been allowed to sleep on because his wife was allergic. Mary C. was moving to Houston and wished to trade a freezer full of deer sausage for a set of good tires to fit a 1988 Chrysler New Yorker.

The two-lane highway took him past the lake and the end-is-near Bible verses. There was the odd house or country store, but it was mostly pine forest on each side of the road. Jack was following directions given to him by Wayne Ambrose, the volunteer fire chief. Look for a big pile of highway department gravel off the roadside, Wayne Ambrose had said, and just past that is Rex Echols's place.

Jack saw the gravel and turned into a driveway, steering his truck over the rough, packed red dirt cross-hatched with fallen pine needles. The drive wound through the trees and opened into a small clearing. Jack saw a one-story brown brick house that could have been plucked from the suburbs of Dallas.

Over the door two horseshoes had been mounted sideways, one on top of the other, to form a rounded E. A red Honda Prelude was parked in front.

He rang the doorbell. A young woman with a pile of blonde hair answered. Inside, on a cloudy day, she was wearing sunglasses. The red frames of her glasses matched her jogging pants and jacket, and she looked good enough that Jack could imagine her as the former Baggett Catfish Rodeo Queen. Michael Jackson music played behind her. She said, "Yeah?"

"Mrs. Echols?"

She acted as if the name gave her a headache. "Why?"

Jack told her he was from Continental Centurion. She said she had plenty of insurance.

"I'm here about the drowning," he said.

"What about it?"

"Just a few questions."

"I wasn't here that night. You'll have to talk to Rex."

"I did. I caught him at the Melon Patch, and he said it was okay if I came on out." Her face said she was tuning him out, so Jack took a leap. "I was wondering if there was a boat stored out back, and if I might have a look at it."

"Suit yourself." She shut the door.

Jack zipped his windbreaker against the cold and walked around the house. At its rear was a rectangular swimming pool, covered by a solarium that was attached to the house. He saw a weathered plywood shed at the edge of the back yard.

The shed was unlocked, but it took some effort to swing the doors open. Except for some spider webs and old cans of motor oil, it was empty.

He walked from the shed and saw the woman leaning out of the door to the solarium. She was smiling and waving him over, as if they were friends all of a sudden. "Come here for a minute," she said as he came closer. "I got a question."

Jack crossed the yard and stepped into the solarium.

The woman walked to a chair, where she laid a towel next to a large leather handbag. "Why's an insurance company want to know what happened with that drowning?" she said.

Take a wild guess, Jack wanted to say. "I'll be happy to answer that. But first, you mind telling me if you are Barbara Echols?"

"Everyone calls me Baby."

"Well, Baby, the insurance company wrote a policy on the deceased."

"You mean like the dead person?" She stood by the pool and began to slip out of her jogging suit. "You mean Mingo?"

"That's what I mean," Jack said.

"Wow, I can't believe Mingo had insurance." The pants came off first, dropping to the cement-and-pebble patio with a wiggle of her hips. Underneath she wore a bikini bottom in a kind of radioactive lime color. The Chernobyl Orchards Collection, Jack figured. "So, like, who's getting the money?" She stepped from the puddle of red cloth at her feet, slipped off the jogging suit's jacket, and regarded her reflection in the house's sliding glass door. "Rex says I'm starting to sag." She fiddled with the bathing suit's top. "Do you think I'm starting to sag?"

"As far as I'm concerned," Jack said, "you've repealed the law of gravity."

"Rex can be such a jerk." She looked at the glass door again, turning slightly for a different view. "He thinks he knows everything because he gives jobs to girls with big boobies. I mean, just because you got a dick that don't mean you're Dick Tracy. You know?"

Jack said, "Uh-huh."

"That's what I always say."

"And who could disagree?"

"Whew." Baby gave a stage shimmy. "It's cold out here. Good thing the pool's heated." She dove in, hardly making a splash, then swam the length and back in a smooth crawl. After another lap she rested her arms on the edge of the pool near Jack, stretched her legs behind herself in a leisurely kick, and said, "You never finished telling me."

"You're a good swimmer," Jack said. "Could Mingo swim?"

"Who knows? I mean, the guy played cards night and day. He was so pale, he looked half-dead anyway. So let's talk about the money from the insurance. Who gets it?"

"If and when the company pays ..." He paused, watching her face. "Rex Echols gets the five hundred thousand dollars."

"Jesus!" Baby rolled her head back, looking toward the gray sky through the glass, then came back to Jack. "Rex? Rex gets half a million?"

"It was partner's insurance. Rex was the sole beneficiary."

Baby shook her head, looking as if she wanted to bite something. "Bastard never said a word to me." She swam to a chrome-plated ladder and climbed out of the pool. "Not one damn word." She pulled her towel from the back of the chair, dried herself quickly, and reached into the leather bag.

"Well, it's a community property state," Jack said, "so what's his is yours. But the company's not going to pay until I finish my inquiry." He watched her hunch over the bag. "Which means I have to track down everyone involved. That's one reason I came to you—"

He stopped talking as she stood up straight. In her right hand she held a gun. "Want to kill some bottles?" she said.

Baby Echols could nail empty Budweisers from thirty paces. She lined six of them up on a log, shot all six off, and said to Jack, "Set some more up." Jack looked at her, at the gun, and back at her. Baby had led him on a narrow path to a clearing, maybe fifty yards from the house, dragging a box of empty bottles behind her.

"Set some more up," Baby said again, "and we'll see how good you are." Jack stood on broken glass while he balanced two Coors, three Miller Lites, and one Heineken on the log. "Don't the neighbors mind?" he asked.

Baby glanced up from her reloading. "Don't have any."

She pushed her palm his way, with a chrome-plated .22 revolver in it. Jack took the gun, steadied his right arm with his left, and fired six times. Four bottles were left standing.

"Let me see that." Baby reloaded, aimed, and fired. Three shots hit three bottles, but two shots missed the last one. She lowered the gun, walked to the log, and blew it apart from six inches away. "That way," she told Jack, "you don't miss."

Jack's ears were ringing. "I'll try to remember that."

Baby looked down the path toward the house. "You want something to drink?"

"Nothing like shooting to work up a man's thirst."

Jack noticed that she reloaded before putting the gun back in her bag.

He let her walk ahead of him. Just before they reached the front door of the house Jack said, "One of the reasons I came out here was to talk to Bobby Slater. I heard he might be here today."

She stopped, turned toward him, and did everything but bare her teeth. "Who told you that?"

"I've been in touch with some friends of his."

"Like who?"

"Friends who are worried about him. Like you are, I would guess."

She shifted the bag, looked away for a moment, then came back to Jack with eyes hard. "You can't prove nothing."

"What are you talking about?"

"Come around here talking about me and Bobby. Next thing you want is money to keep quiet, right?"

Jack held up a hand. "Slow down."

"But you can't prove one fucking thing."

"Look, we already talked about this. Somebody drowned. Bobby Slater was listed as a witness. That's my interest here. If you and Bobby are hot tub buddies, congratulations. I couldn't care less."

Baby gazed past him with a twisted smile. Jack couldn't imagine what was in her head. He got his answer when she stepped around him, pulled the gun from her bag, and fired. The left headlight on Jack's truck shattered. A second shot hit something, but he didn't know what. She fired again and blew out the light on the right side.

She turned back toward him, lowered the gun, and said, "Not one fucking thing, man."

His truck looked like a blind man. The remains of the headlights lay on the ground, nothing but big silver flakes now. "You know," Jack said, "I was going to replace those old things anyway."

It was growing dark by the time Jack got back to town, running on parking lights. Halfway there the truck had started to overheat. He found Wayne Ambrose in his Fina station watching *Wheel of Fortune*. Wayne checked the headlights for a few seconds and announced, "Gonna need some new ones." After about five minutes under the hood he said, "Big old chunk outta that radiator. Let's pull her into the bay."

Jack stood in the garage, getting cold while Wayne did his work. Every now and then Wayne would have to drop his tools and pump a customer's gas. One who stopped in for a fill-up was Loyce Slapp in his white cruiser, a Crown Victoria with the blue lights on top and a star on the door. Jack saw him pointing at the truck and talking to Wayne, then nodding.

"What was the sheriff wanting to know?" Jack asked when Wayne came back.

"He was just asking what happened to you."

"That's it?"

"He wanted to know if you'd have to spend the night."

"I'm wondering the same thing"

Wayne walked away from the truck toward the phone. "You're gonna need a new radiator. Let's make some calls and see."

It took four or five tries, but Wayne finally found a junkyard in Marshall with a radiator for a Ford pickup.

The dealership in Tyler also had one, but Marshall was closer. Not that it made any difference, because both of them were about to close for the day. "I'll run over first thing in the morning," Wayne said. "Until then ... welcome to Baggett."

"You know this Baby Echols?" Jack asked. Wayne Ambrose was driving his Fina tow truck on the highway east of town, giving Jack a lift.

"I was out to their house a couple of months ago when they had a small fire," Wayne said. "Burning log on the couch."

"Has to be a story there."

"The way I understand it, Mr. and Mrs. Echols were having a disagreement, and he was next to the fireplace. Mr. Echols grabbed a log with the tongs and tossed it . . . Well, Mr. Flippo, here you go."

They were in front of the Heart-o-the-Pines Lodge. It was a tourist court, and Jack figured it had looked pretty good as recently as 1965. He stepped down from the tow truck. Wayne said he'd call him with news about the radiator in the morning, and drove off with a wave.

Jack glanced across the highway at a collection of empty plywood sheds. A ragged banner that said BAGGETT FLEA MARKET EVERY SAT flapped in the wind. He turned to inspect his home for the night. Above him a neon sign buzzed and flickered in the near dusk. Green water with a coat of dead leaves and pine needles filled the swimming pool halfway.

The lodge itself was a one-story run of a dozen brick units that flaked gray paint and trailed off toward a stand of trees. He saw one car, a rusted heap of a Buick, at the far end of the parking lot.

Jack pulled open a plate-glass door and stepped into a dim, unoccupied lobby-office. Two sagging chairs with worn plaid upholstery faced an old TV that had a snowy picture and no sound. An empty coffeemaker sat on a small table. Above it, a handwritten sign had been tacked to the wall: FREE CUP FOR EACH COSTUMER LIMIT ONE.

"Hello," Jack called. "Mr. Bates?"

He rang a bell on the counter and within seconds a small man emerged from behind a wall. He had a white smile against dark skin and black hair thick with brilliantine. "Oh, yes," he said. "A lovely guest room for you?" He placed a registration card on the counter and handed Jack a Holiday Inn pen.

Halfway through his name Jack stopped writing when the man gazed past his shoulder and said, "Oh, there must be problems." Jack turned and looked through the glass front door. Loyce Slapp's patrol car was stopped under the flea market banner. After half a minute the car pulled away.

"What I'd like to do before I check in," Jack said, "if you don't mind, is take a look at a couple of rooms first."

"Yes, yes."

As they made a crooked path across the parking lot, dodging chuckholes full of rainwater, the man said his name was Mr. Patel and he had come from India six months before to buy the Heart-o-the-Pines from his cousin Ranjit. "We have decorated it very nice."

"I can tell."

"This room is most pleasant," Mr. Patel said, unlocking number 11. When they were inside he gestured as if Jack were Robin Leach with a camera crew. "The bed, very large as you see, we have arranged with most modern colors."

Jack walked to the bed and looked at the painting of bluebonnets over the headboard. He pushed on the mattress. It appeared to have been passed down through several generations of carnival fat men.

"Television is absolutely free with no charge to the costumer," Mr. Patel said. "The closet, very large as you see, will contain all your luggage."

Jack's luggage was a paper bag with a toothbrush, toothpaste, and shampoo, which he had picked up when Wayne Ambrose stopped at the Bag-Mart on the way. He looked around and nodded. "Very impressive."

The window at the back wall held the air conditioner, and the sash was bolted in place. Jack turned to Mr. Patel and said, "May I have a moment in the bathroom?"

"Certainly. You will find it very pleasant to the eye."

Jack closed the door, ran some water, and checked the window there. It opened onto the back of the unit, and was about two feet by three feet. Plenty large, he figured as he unlatched it.

"Lovely quarters," he said as he came out of the bathroom. Mr. Patel beamed. "But," Jack said, "I'd like to see number ten."

"Number ten, sir?"

"The room next door. I'd like to see it."

"Certainly." Mr. Patel pulled a ring full of keys from his pocket. "If you will come with me this way."

Number 10 was much the same, except that the painting over the bed showed a sad clown with one tear rolling down his cheek, washing a trail in the makeup. "I'll take this one," Jack said. "Better art."

There was a pizza place in Baggett that delivered, so that was Jack's dinner. Entertainment was provided by a made-for-TV movie about a woman with amnesia who's taken home from the hospital by a guy who claims he's her husband but really isn't, and she doesn't snap to this until she's fallen in love with him. A Hershey bar Jack had bought earlier at the Bag-Mart became his late-night snack.

At just after ten Jack stepped from his room and stood shivering beneath the porch light above his door. Only one other unit at the lodge appeared to be occupied. A couple of trucks rumbled by on the highway. In the weak light the puddles in the empty parking lot looked like lard. He poked the tip of his shoe into one of them and broke a thin sheet of ice.

Jack spent about five minutes outside, just taking some fresh air, you would think if you happened to be watching from somewhere like the flea market sheds across the street. Then back to his room, time for bed. He found an extra blanket and pillow in the closet, took two towels from the bathroom, and formed them on the bed into the sprawling Z-shape of a man sleeping on his side. The ice bucket became his head, the bedside Bible a shoulder blade.

He covered it all with the bedspread, turned out the lamps, and adjusted the brightness knob on the TV down so that the screen gave off the faintest of glows. A night-light for little ice-bucket head. It was just like his mom tucking him, Jack thought. Tucking him in and saying a prayer, If I should die before I wake I pray the Lord my soul to take.

Playing a hunch was a form of faith, Jack thought as he crawled out the bathroom window. You had to believe in your hunches the same way people in South Texas some-times believed the figure of the Virgin Mary could appear in a tortilla. No way to prove it true or not, you either bought it or you didn't. And if you bought it, you got down on your knees to weep before a number three com-bination plate or you squirmed out the back of a motel into the cold.

Getting out was harder work than Jack had thought, the jump down longer. He landed hard, his right foot twisting inward. When he stepped with his left foot he found air. Jack tumbled backward, rolling six or seven feet downhill into a tangle of dead vines.

He tried to focus and couldn't because there was noth-ing to focus on. It was too dark to see his hands in front of him. He crawled up the slope, digging toeholds in the muck and grabbing at the vines to keep from sliding back down. At the top he stood and felt his way, fingertips over the cold wall with its scaling paint, until he found the bathroom window of room 11.

The sill was two feet above his head. Jack hooked his fingers over it and pulled. His legs moved fast but his shoes slipped on the brick like tires spinning in mud. He stopped to catch his breath, thinking that cat burglar was never going to be a career option.

Jack kicked off his shoes and tried again. Fingers on the sill, toes in the mortar gaps between the bricks, not exactly the Human Fly but he managed to hook an elbow over the top. He got the window open without much effort and crawled in, wheelbarrowing across the sink and toilet.

His feet cleared the window and he stood, wet socks on the tile floor. He ran his hands over his clothes. Mud was smeared thick as cake icing. He filled the sink with warm water and thawed his numb fingers.

It was close to midnight when he settled himself onto a straight-backed wooden chair, a blanket over him and his feet propped on the bed. He could sleep in this position, but not too soundly.

Jack dozed for several hours, waking every twenty to thirty minutes cold and stiff, his back beginning to ache. He floated in and out of dreams that didn't hold him. In one he was driving a car with his ex-wife at his side. He steered it off the road and into a ditch full of chocolate syrup and swarming with snapping turtles. Jack stayed awake for a while trying to dope that one out.

In another dream he was with his father, watching pro wrestlers. No mystery there: The wrestling matches were the clearest memory he had of his father.

They had gone every Friday night when Jack was a kid. Down to the shabby white barn of a building south of downtown Dallas, big neon letters on the front, lit up red—SPORTATORIUM. His father, still in dirty gray khakis from work, would have a Schlitz in one hand and a dime-store cigar in the other. Between matches he discoursed on the finer points of tag-teaming and the sleeper hold.

They sat in banged-up metal folding chairs at ringside, close enough to get hit with flying sweat. Gray smoke hung in the hot white light above the ring. The air smelled of cigarettes, popcorn, body odor, and urinal cakes. Some nights the crowd should have been caged. To Jack it was the greatest place in the world.

The old man's favorite thing to watch was the foiled body slam. It worked the same way every time: One wrestler looks to be out cold on the mat. The other one climbs to the top rope at the nearest corner. He launches himself up and out, an overweight guy in his bathing suit about to do a wicked bellyflop on his helpless foe.

But the one on the mat somehow sees him coming. He rolls out of the way at the last possible instant. The flying wrestler lands dead, like a sack of flour dropped from the rooftop. His opponent flips him over and pins him, end of match.

Jack's old man hacks out a laugh and follows with his own ritual. He places the Schlitz can on the floor with such care you'd think it was the family crystal. Cigar butt dies under the heel of a Red Wing boot. Big hands, lined with grease that never washes out, are cupped around his mouth. Then the commentary, loud as a man with one lung could manage, aimed at the loser as he rises and staggers off: "Next time, shithead, think twice."

Around three o'clock Jack could take no more of the Heart-o-the-Pines chair. He stood, rubbed the part of his back he could reach, and stared toward the bed. Imagining how it would feel to sink into the mattress and pull the blanket over him, to drop into the black softness and close his eyes, like falling in love but without all the problems.

He wasn't sure how long he had been standing there when something moved across the front window, a shadow floating from left to right. Jack went to the curtains and parted them with a fingertip. He could see the back of a man, better than six feet tall, with a long, heavy jacket and a watch cap. The man raised one gloved hand to the porch light in front of room 10 next door and began to unscrew the bulb. There was the brittle squeak of metal against metal and the light blinked off.

Jack could make out only a silhouette as the man turned, raised a leg, and crashed a foot into the door to room 10. Then he vanished.

"Mr. Patel won't like that," Jack said. He opened his own door and slipped out, taking his chair with him. The cold of the concrete walkway stung his bare feet. He stepped next to the doorway to room 10 and peered in.

He could see it all in the thin blue light from the TV. The man was hunched over the bed, lifting some kind of club and bringing it down with a grunt and a soft thud. He did it again, then a third time. Real legs beneath the bedspread would have been broken, real ribs shattered. Jack wondered how long it would take him to understand he was beating the hell out of some towels.

After the fifth or sixth blow the man reached for the bedspread and yanked it away. Jack moved from the doorway and put his back against the outside wall. He heard "Shit!" and then the shattering of the plastic ice bucket.

Jack grasped his chair by two of its legs, raised it, and

listened as the ice bucket took another blow. There was silence, then hard breathing and the sound of heavy shoes across the carpet.

He swung the chair at the first blur of movement in the doorway. A nice, smooth arc, nose-high, like going for a fastball out of the strike zone. The man tried to raise his arm but wasn't quick enough. The chair broke across his face. He fell to the right. Something hit the sidewalk with an almost musical ringing. Jack looked down to see a length of pipe bounce a couple of times on the concrete before it fell over the six-inch ledge and into the parking lot.

The man was on his hands and knees. Jack hadn't glimpsed a face yet. In his right hand he still held one leg of the chair, which he swung and splintered on the back of the man's shoulders. The man buckled but didn't collapse.

Jack couldn't see the pipe, but he leaped from the sidewalk in its direction. His feet landed on a patch of ice. He slid, caught his fall with one hand, turned, and ended up on his knees. The pipe was right in front of him. He grabbed it, dropped it, grabbed it again, and stood.

The man had gained his feet and was stumbling down the sidewalk away from Jack, one hand over his face and the other straight in front of him as if to feel his way. He was a good forty feet away now, running by the next-to-last room at the Heart-o-the-Pines. A few more seconds and he would reach the end of the sidewalk and vanish into the trees.

Jack held the pipe as if he were about to swat a backhand on the tennis court. He flung it as hard as he could, aiming for the head.

The pipe whirled like a helicopter blade toward its target. Jack tried to watch it go but lost it in the dark. His eyes darted back to the man, who was running now past the last room's window. The window shattered beside him. The man staggered to the end of the sidewalk and seemed to dive into the night.

Jack cupped his hands, raised them to his mouth, and yelled, "Next time, shithead, think twice."

16 Mr. Patel arrived near-breathless from his sprint out of the office. He wore pajamas and carried a flashlight. "Get the light off me," ordered Jack.

"I hear the breaking of glass," he said.

"Among other things."

"I am hoping it is a nightmare, but with all this commotion, I have telephoned the authorities."

Jack pointed in the direction of the last room. "That window's gone."

Mr. Patel shined the flashlight and said, "Oh, no." Jack walked to room 10 and ran his hands over the doorjamb. "You've got some damage here, too."

"Oh, this is very, very bad." Mr. Patel shook his head. "My cousin, Ranjit, never spoke of such things. Very quiet place is what Ranjit said." He cradled the remains of the dead chair as if it were the body of a loved one. "Oh, this is very bad."

Jack stepped onto the carpet of his room to get his feet off the cold sidewalk. "I have to ask you a favor, kind of a guest service," he said. "Could you go around back and grab my shoes?"

He had his shoes back, plus a dry pair of black socks courtesy of Mr. Patel, by the time a deputy from the Baggett Sheriff's Office drove into the parking lot. The deputy was eighteen or nineteen, with a burr haircut and acne, and a wad of tobacco in his cheek. He was so short and thin he looked like a little kid dressed up as a cop.

After hearing Jack's story he walked to the end of the sidewalk, his shoes crunching on the broken glass, and swept the woods a couple of times with his flashlight. "Sir, what I think I'll do on this here one." He stopped to spit brown juice into a stained styrofoam cup he carried. "What I think I'll do is call the sheriff."

Half an hour later there was a hard knock and a soft voice saying, "It's Sheriff Slapp."

Jack opened his door. The sheriff looked him up and down like a bank president eyeballing the janitor who wants to marry his daughter. Jack wore Mr. Patel's socks and a blanket that he had wrapped around himself. "The owner's washing my clothes," he said.

Loyce Slapp had on a red and green flannel shirt, brown corduroy trousers, black leather gloves, unscuffed all-weather boots, and a buttery suede overcoat. His hair had been gelled and combed. He had shaved and, from the smell of things, slapped on plenty of Paco Rabanne. It was 4:35 A.M.

"I need to talk to my deputy first," he said. "Don't you think of moving till I get back. Don't you go anywhere."

Jack returned to the bed. He was drinking an RC Cola from the Heart-o-the-Pines vending machine and watching a ladies' bowling tournament on TV. "And give up all this?" he said.

The sheriff left. Five minutes later he was back in the room again. The first thing Jack noticed was the length of pipe in his left hand. Loyce Slapp stood a few feet from the door and started talking.

"What?" Jack put a hand to his ear.

The sheriff turned off the bowling tournament. The screen went dark except for a shrinking dot of light at the center. Jack said, "Now I'll never know if she picked up that spare."

"My deputy thinks we should charge you."

Jack rolled off the bed and stood. "Who thinks that? Barney Fife Junior out there? I doubt it."

"Destruction of private property. Malicious mischief. Must be four, five hundred dollars' worth of damage here. Maybe six."

Jack laughed. "Now I'm really scared."

"My deputy also thinks you made a false statement to a sworn peace officer."

The blanket started to slip. Jack wrapped it tighter around himself. "What do you say, let's get your deputy in here and listen to his story, no prompting from you."

The sheriff held the pipe with his arm hanging straight down. He tapped a slow beat against the side of his leg. Man had some mirrored shades on, Jack was thinking, he could play the prison guard in a drive-in movie. Loyce Slapp said, "He had a long night, I sent him home."

Jack hadn't expected that. He looked toward the front window. The curtains were closed. He brought his eyes back to the sheriff. "I know you have a different way of doing things in this county. But I'm thinking maybe some-body should be looking for the dude who tried to kill me."

Loyce Slapp stared at Jack and tapped the tire tool against his leg.

Jack said, "Your thoughts, Sheriff?"

"You have no description of him. No license plate number. No witnesses. No motive."

Jack waited for him to go on, sure the sheriff would now accuse him of holding something back. Say some-thing like, Was that a jealous husband coming after you? Or, You got some nasty debts that need to be paid? Jack would say no, and the sheriff would say if Jack couldn't come up with something, there was nothing he could do, nowhere he could take this investigation, end of discus-sion. He'd throw a few tough-lawman looks at Jack, then drive off, the way Jack figured.

But Loyce Slapp said, "This sheriff thinks you're mak-ing the whole thing up."

Jack nodded. "Well, this sheriff must've gone overtime in the tanning bed and got his brain cooked."

Loyce Slapp raised the pipe and studied it. He stood between Jack and the door. "You can't say who this assailant's supposed to be? Do I have that right, now? You can't give me a name. Can't say why he was here."

"I know why he was here. So do you. He was here to bust me up."

"All this stuff you don't know. But for some reason you knew enough to sneak out of your room and sneak into another one. You knew enough to get cute."

Jack didn't answer. He was about to say, Cut the crap, Sheriff. About to tell him, You know, and I know you know. But he watched Loyce Slapp's free hand move to his hip, beneath the suede overcoat. "Could be you just went crazy," the sheriff said, voice dropping, mud-colored eyes narrowing. "Kicking in doors and breaking windows, stuff that nutballs do all the time."

"That's not what happened." Jack was backed into a corner with nothing to defend himself with and nowhere to go, how dumb could you get? Never saw it coming until too late. His hunches had walked out on him. Now a cracker with a manicure had him cold. "You're way off base," was all he could say.

The sheriff's hand stopped under the coat about where a holster would be. Freezing cold outside and his upper lip was gleaming sweat. "Oh, those crazy people, they do all sorts of stuff," he said. "They see things nobody else does, they have fits, they get violent. Claim spaceships are sending them signals and nonsense. Say one of them had a big old pipe like this here, he might even come after a peace officer. Peace officer wouldn't have a choice but to defend himself."

Fear was in Jack's chest, a clutch of cold bony fingers. He couldn't swallow. The blanket fell away.

"See, you even look like a crazy man," Loyce Slapp said. "Butt naked except for some socks."

"You'd never get away with it." Jack wondered how he could make the sheriff believe that when he didn't buy it himself.

"With what? Defending myself?" The sheriff seemed to focus on Jack's chest. The heater stopped blowing and the room went quiet. Jack didn't know if Loyce Slapp was figuring the angles or gathering his nerve. He watched the bulge of hand under the coat. "I had to kill a crazy man once before," the sheriff whispered. "No other way to put him down, he was so wild. People came up and thanked me for it later."

They stared at each other. The only sound was the two of them breathing. "You see," Loyce Slapp finally said, "most everyone's afraid of a crazy man."

Someone knocked on the door three times. "Good morning?" a voice called from outside.

"Come in," Jack yelled. Thinking, Doesn't matter who it is, anything's an improvement.

The door opened a foot. The voice said, "Your clothes are very nice and clean, sir." Mr. Patel stuck his head in. He looked at Jack, then at Loyce Slapp, then back at Jack. "Do I interrupt something?"

"Come in." Jack grabbed the blanket from the floor and wrapped it around his waist. "Come on in and set a spell, as they say in East Texas. Right, Sheriff? That what they say, set a spell?"

The sheriff eased his right hand from under the jacket. Mr. Patel set Jack's clothes, folded into a neat stack, on the end of the bed. "Sit down," Jack said, "and tell Sheriff Loyce here how you bought this place from your cousin. It's quite a story, Sheriff. All the way from India, just to run the Heart-o-the-Pines."

"I've heard it," Loyce Slapp said. His eyes burned into Jack.

"Well, I'm sure he has plenty other tales." Jack began to pull on his clothes. "Don't you? Sit down and tell us about yourself, Mr. Patel. Start with your childhood."

Mr. Patel smiled and shook his head. "That is very

nice, sir, but I have much work awaiting for me back at the office." He gestured out the door with a fluttering hand. "Insurance filings for the damages and such."

Jack buttoned his shirt. "Maybe I'll come hang out at the office, too. Enjoy some of that complimentary coffee." He tucked in his shirttail and zipped his pants. "How about that, Mr. Patel? Since the sheriff and I seem to be through talking."

He tied his shoes, stood, and started to walk toward the door on shaky legs. Loyce Slapp didn't move. They faced each other two feet apart. Jack stepped around him and said, "Next time, Sheriff."

By midmorning the new radiator was in his truck and he was on his way back to Dallas. About fifty miles out of Baggett he let himself start thinking about what had almost happened.

Jack saw himself dead on the motel floor, his blood soaking into the rug as Justice of the Peace Webb Carroll showed up with his assistant Jim Dandy to investigate. Imagined his body carted over to the Earl D. Yost Funeral Home, turned to ashes in the only crematorium in the tri-county area, then poured into an urn.

They probably would have put it on the shelf right next to Mingo No-Bird's and waited for a loved one to come claim it. And waited, Jack thought, and waited and waited some more.

"Pick it up," Tony Angel said. "Hump it. You're about to lose him. You proud of yourself now, Mitch, now that you lost him? The whole project on the line here and you lost him, thank you very fucking much."

Mitch steered his black Ford van south on Hillcrest, trying to change lanes in heavy traffic and keep sight of the blue pickup truck he was tailing. "Man, this stuff looks so easy on TV."

"Enough." Tony jerked a thumb to the right. "Pull over."

They were in the stretch by Southern Methodist University that had signals at nearly every corner. There were students on bicycles, sorority girls in convertibles, and country club wives in their baby Benzes. Drivers darted in and out of parking lots.

"Gotta have a helicopter to follow somebody in here," Mitch said. He passed a car on the right, and the lane ahead opened for three or four blocks with nothing but green lights. He sped up to forty-five. "Awreet." Mitch slapped the dash. "We're rollin' now."

"You frigging deaf? I said pull over." Tony grabbed the steering wheel and tugged. The van veered to the right. Mitch yanked it back to the left, too hard. It crossed into the next lane and came within inches of sideswiping a Lexus. The Lexus swerved into oncoming traffic, where it clipped the rear quarter-panel of a Ford Taurus.

Mitch, weaving back to the right, saw a few frames of the wreck in his side mirror—two cars hitting and spinning, a quick sparkle of flying glass and plastic shards catching the sun, the other drivers scrambling to get out of the way. "Holy shit." He turned to Tony. "Look at what you did, man. You're crazy."

Tony glared at Mitch. "Pull over, you fucking mental case, and let me drive." He reached for the steering wheel again. Mitch never slowed the van down, just batted Tony's hand away with his forearm.

"It's my van," Mitch told him. He watched Tony's hands, making sure he didn't try another grab at the wheel. Just watching and waiting, ready to show Tony who was in control here, until the corner of his eye picked up something big and yellow.

Mitch turned and saw a parked delivery truck straight ahead. Its back door was like a wall coming at them.

He jumped on the brakes. The tires screamed and the van nosed down. Tony flew from his seat, slamming into the dashboard. Mitch cut the wheel left. The van skidded sideways, leaning, feeling for an instant as if it were on two tires. The yellow wall sailed up to the passenger window and stopped. The van rocked, then was still, and the noise had gone.

"Christ almighty," Tony moaned. He lay on the floor in front of his seat with his feet in the air and his head down by the heater duct.

Mitch opened his door and stepped from the van. Three blocks back the two wrecked cars, strewn across a couple of lanes, had drawn a crowd. He walked around the front of the van, afraid to see what had happened to the other side. His heart felt as if it had turned a couple of flips. He closed his eyes for a few seconds, opened them, and looked. The body of the van was an eyelash from the truck's bumper. He could not have run his little finger through the space between them. "Man," was all he could say. "Man."

A blast from the van's horn smacked his ear and gave him a jump. He looked through the windshield to see Tony in the driver's seat. Tony hit the horn again and waved at him to step aside. "Don't do it," Mitch yelled. "No room. Wait till they move the truck."

He saw Tony reach for the shift lever and heard the transmission clank. The van began to inch forward. Mitch stood in front of it, shaking his head. "Come on, Tony, wait."

Tony blew the horn once more and kept rolling. Mitch braced himself against the front end, stepped back when he had to, and braced himself again. "Please, Tony, no." He started to cry. The van was the only thing besides fire that Mitch really loved. Ten years old with a perfect paint job, maybe a little hard to start lately, but a beautiful gleaming black, you couldn't look at it on a sunny day without wearing shades. His tears dropped onto the shiny hood. Any second there would be the horrible squeal of the truck's bumper digging into the van's skin, to Mitch like a big hand clawing a hole out of his belly.

And then it was clear. Mitch couldn't believe it. He stood in the street, looking from the truck's bumper to the van and back, thinking he'd just seen a magic act, a Houdini bit.

"Get the fuck in," Tony ordered. He opened the passenger door, and Mitch climbed in. Tony punched the gas and the door slammed shut on its own as they roared away. "Next time," Tony said, "save us all a lot of grief and do what I say."

Mitch studied his boots. "Sorry, man."

Tony ran a red light and took the van to fifty. "Remember who's giving the orders here. When I say 'jump,' you start looking for a frigging cliff."

"I know, I know." Mitch searched his jacket pocket for his lighter.

They were up to fifty-five now. "Repeat the words after me." Tony whipped around a car in front of him. "Say the words, I am nothing but a production assistant."

"Oh, man, Tony . . . " He found the lighter, scratched the wheel with his thumb, and gazed at the flame.

"Say it. Right now. Say it, Mitch. A production assistant, that's all I am."

Mitch released the lighter's plastic tab and the flame vanished. He sighed. "I am a production assistant."

"And the word 'no' does not come from my mouth."

"Not from my mouth."

"Very good. Thank you. Asshole!" Tony braked hard as a slow-moving car pulled in front of him. He dodged left, knocking Mitch into the door, then right, throwing

Mitch the other way. "Hey this is nothing when you done the Garden State Parkway, know what I'm saying?"

Mitch played with his lighter.

"Will you look at that." Tony slowed the van and pointed toward a Shell station. The blue pickup truck was parked at the pumps. "Watch and learn, Mitch. See how it's done."

They stopped at the curb. A few minutes later the truck left the gas station, went three blocks farther south on Hillcrest, and turned right on Normandy. "Let me tell you something," Tony said as he followed. "Don't let nobody ever steer you different, Mitch. Art is—will you put down the lighter and listen? Art is hard work. Art is sacrifice. Hey, when I was with Caesar's, we—all right, he's doing something here."

The truck stopped in front of a two-story house. "Look at this, this is beautiful," Tony said. "There's a school right across the street with its own parking, everything. That's where we'll wait."

Tony drove the van into the school lot and backed into a space, giving them a full view of the house and the truck. "Absolutely what the doctor ordered," he said. "We got the bastard in our sights now."

Jack double-checked the address. Just back from his Baggett County adventure that morning, he had gone straight to his office and spent time at his computer. Driver's license records had given him 3585 Normandy Avenue.

The house at 3585 was clapboard with two floors and big windows, probably sixty years old, subdivided now into three or four apartments. Its white paint looked reasonably fresh, and ivy trailed up the porch columns. Other small, neat apartment houses lined that side of the street. On the other side a red brick school took up the block.

It was a tidy but plain neighborhood, an odd pocket of University Park. Go a quarter-mile south or west and there were the homes of law firm partners and bank presidents. But this was the lower end of an upper-crust town—a place for college kids, the just-married, and, Jack hoped, one bartender named Sally Danvers.

He left his truck, stepping into the early afternoon sunshine. A sharp north wind had swept away all the rain and clouds from the night before, leaving a deep blue dome of sky. It was the kind of day that could make you feel happy if you weren't careful.

The mailboxes attached to the side of the house listed no names, so Jack started knocking at apartments. Nobody was home at the two on the bottom floor. He climbed the stairs to the balcony porch and found one door. It was open a few inches.

Jack knocked, called "Hello," and got no answer. Through the opening he could see the television. The end credits were rolling on an episode of *The Beverly Hillbillies*. "Hello," Jack said again. "Anybody home?"

The place was quiet except for the man on TV singing, *. . . to have a heapin' helpin' of their hospitality*. Jack nudged the door with his foot and stepped into the room. "Hello?" The TV advised, *Take your shoes off*.

The living room had white walls and wood floors stained dark. Two round wicker tables flanked a futon couch. Shelves made of pine planks on milk crates held the small TV and a modest stereo.

To the right the room opened onto a kitchen, big

enough for a butcher-block table and two stools. An ashtray had been overturned on the table, scattering ashes and lipstick-smeared butts. One of the stools lay on its side.

He moved down the hallway, the wood floor creaking under his shoes, and came to a dark bathroom. Jack reached around the doorframe, running his fingers over the wall until he touched a switch. He flipped it. The exhaust fan began to hum.

Another try found the bathroom light. He waited a couple of beats before stepping into the doorway. The tile was pink, the walls gray. A razor, some shampoo, bottles of bath oil, and tubes of cream formed a ragged column along the rim of the tub. On the toilet tank a clear glass vase held a spray of dried flowers. A pink bath towel, damp to the touch, hung on a chromed bar.

On the bare tile floor the shards of a white china cup lay in a pool of black coffee. Jack knelt and put a finger into the coffee. It was still warm.

He followed the hall to the back of the apartment. The first room he came to was open. Inside were stacks of cardboard boxes, each taped shut. Jack stepped back to the hallway and over to the next room.

He listened for a moment at the door and heard nothing. His hand went to the glass knob, turned, pushed. The door swung open without a rub or a squeak.

The room had bare, cream-colored walls. A long pine dresser stood at one end. One of its drawers was open, spilling lacy underwear. Next to the bed was a small table with a lamp, a phone, a couple of books, and a brown druggist's bottle of pills.

Six full windows lined two of its walls. Wooden venetian blinds hung in each one, casting blades of shadow and light that fell on Sally Danvers.

She lay in the middle of a double bed, on her back, nude. Her head was turned to one side, her hair in a small fan on the pillow. A sheet the color of sea foam covered her from her hips down. Her chest rose and fell with the rhythm of sleep.

Jack saw himself turning and leaving, imagined the gentle closing of the door behind him and the soiled feeling of having seen something he shouldn't have. But he didn't go. He took a step forward, then another, and in a moment found himself almost to the foot of the bed.

The whiteness of her skin, where the sun hit it, had the hint of blue beneath. Her breasts were small with nipples the color of old pennies. A tease of black pubic hair peeked from the edge of the sheet.

He could hear her breathing and could see the pulse in her neck. Watching her touched the ache inside him like a tongue probing a bad tooth.

Jack did not know how long he had been standing there when the front door to the apartment slammed. He left the room and walked down the hallway as quietly as he could. In the kitchen a woman used a wet cloth to wipe up the mess from the overturned ashtray, her back to him. "Hello," Jack said.

"Hi," she said, not looking up.

"I'm Jack."

"How you doin', Jack?" The woman had blonde hair with dark roots and wore a gray sweatsuit. Jack, watching her use one hand to rake the butts into the ashtray, thought the fingernails looked familiar.

"Doing okay," he said. "How about you?"

"Be better as soon as I get this mess cleaned up." She wiped the table clean, then turned to face him. "I'm April."

"As in April Showers."

"Yeah." She inspected Jack. "You a customer at the Melon Patch?"

"Been there once or twice."

"Okay," she said, drawing the word out, still looking at him a little sideways.

Jack pointed to the back of the apartment. "I stopped by to see Sally but she's still asleep."

"I think she was up late." April rinsed her cleaning rag in the kitchen sink. "It's her day off. She'll probably be up soon. You want some coffee while you wait?"

"Love some."

"I'll make a fresh—oh, crap, coffee. That's another mess." April took her rag toward the bathroom. "Be right back."

Jack watched her go down the hall, then heard her say, "Oh, you're up . . . Sally, honey, I dropped a cup in here, I'm sorry."

"That's okay." Sleep was still in her voice.

"I'm gonna make some coffee for your friend," April said. "Then I gotta run"

"What friend?" he heard Sally say.

18 Jack answered the question as Sally walked into the room. "This friend," he said, tapping his chest with two fingers. "The one who went to East Texas yesterday on your advice. Went there and asked a woman uncomfortable questions. Turns out she likes to shoot things."

Sally was wearing jeans and a man's long-sleeved dress shirt. She showed Jack a face he couldn't read, then went to the kitchen and poured herself some coffee. "Baby still likes the guns?" She leaned against the counter, warming her hands on the mug, and looked Jack up and down. "I don't see any holes in you."

"I asked her about Bobby Slater and she killed my radiator." He lifted his shoulders. "Could have been worse. Could have been the gas tank. Could have been me."

Sally nodded. "Bobby taught her to shoot. He used to be a cop, back in his hometown, so he knows his way around guns . . . Why are you staring at me like that?"

Jack cleared his throat, searching for an answer and coming up empty, when April Showers saved him. "All done," she said, walking in with the rag and pieces of the broken cup. "Sorry about the mess."

"It's okay," Sally told her.

"I'm in the bathroom, right? I've got a cup of coffee in there, too, everything's cool till I drop it. I come out here to get a paper towel to clean it up with, okay, but first I want to get a cigarette. So I reach into my purse and the first thing I see's my light bill. And I'm like, oh shit, they said if I didn't mail it today they was gonna cut me off. That's when I knock over the ashtray."

"You had to run out and mail the payment," Sally said.

"First I had to find someplace to buy a stamp."

Sally looked at Jack. "April's roommate has a boyfriend she doesn't like. When he's at her apartment April stays here."

"He walks around the apartment with nothin' but this jockstrap on." April made a face. "Like I'm supposed to get off on this. I'm goin' to my roommate, 'Julie, how about dumpin' this creep?' I'm about to move out of that place, I don't care if my name is on the lease. I'll break it, I don't care."

"Bring me a copy of your lease," Jack said. "I'll take a look at it. Maybe there's a way out for you, get your deposit back."

"That's right," Sally said, sighting him over the rim of her cup. "A lawyer."

"Cool," April said. "Hey, I gotta run." She kissed Sally on the cheek. "I been late two days in a row and Rex is all pissed about it."

When she was gone the room was quiet until Jack said, "I never would have figured you two for pals."

"What kind of snot thing is that to say?"

"You two just seem different, that's all."

"We help each other out. You have a problem with that?"

Jack held up both hands. "I think that's great."

"There's nothing wrong with April. The kind of life she's had, she's done okay."

"I'm sure you're right."

"It's been hard for her every step."

Jack apologized and retreated to the kitchen to pour himself more coffee. He gave her some time to cool down, then came back and changed the subject. "Can we get back to talking about Bobby Slater?" She drank her coffee, no answer. "Are you good friends," he said, "or *real* good friends?"

Sally blinked a couple of times. "What difference does it make?"

Jack walked back to the stool. "To me, a big difference. Because last night I almost got seriously injured, twice. And then there's Baby Echols, who starts blazing away at the mere mention of Bobby Slater. So I'm thinking I need a program for this game." He waited for her to answer.

"There's a lot about this I don't know."

"I'll take what you have."

She looked away again. "It could take a while."

"Lucky for us my calendar's clear today."

Sally placed her cup on the counter. "It's too dark in here." She went to the big windows behind the couch and raised the shade on each. Light filled that end of the room, hitting the floor in bright skewed rectangles. "Give me a few minutes," she said, going down the hallway without glancing back.

Jack turned off the television and toured the room. There wasn't much to see. On the shelves he glanced at some books on dancing and a few family photographs where everybody looked happy. A few dozen tapes were lined up next to the stereo, mostly rock and jazz with some old stage musicals thrown in. *The Music Man. Oklahoma! South Pacific.* Jack began to whistle "There Is Nothing Like a Dame."

Five minutes and she was back, still in jeans but with her hair brushed and the wrinkled shirt gone, replaced by a soft v-neck sweater with nothing beneath it that Jack could tell. "Okay," she said, getting a pack of cigarettes from a kitchen cabinet. "Okay. You want my story, it'll cost you some money."

Jack hadn't expected that one. "It'll what?"

Sally looked straight at him. "If I'm talking, you're buying lunch."

Rex Echols unlocked the front door of his North Dallas house, came inside, and closed it behind him, quiet as a burglar. He moved through the living room and saw what he wanted. The back door made almost no noise as he opened it, and he stepped softly onto the wooden deck. He watched her for a while before saying, "Surprise."

"Jesus!" Baby Echols turned, one hand over her heart. She was in the spa, water bubbling around her, a copy of *Soap Opera Digest* in the other hand. "You scared the shit out of me. What're you doing here?"

Rex smiled. "Can't a man come home to his own house? Come home and see his own beautiful wife? How's the water in there, anyway?"

"You never come home in the afternoon."

"I got a special problem today."

"What kind of problem?"

"I got me a hard-on"—Rex sniffed—"if it hit somebody in the head it'd knock 'em out cold. Be like a smack in the face with a Jimmy Dean sausage."

"Get real, Rex. What're you doing here? Who's watching the Melon Patch?"

Rex said, "You got anything on? Stand up and lemme see." The deck was bordered on two sides by the house, and on the other two by an eight-foot cedar fence. What's the use in having a hot tub, Rex had asked when it was built, if you can't get naked without the neighbors looking? "Stand up," Rex told Baby, "and let me see if you got the cure for this swellin' condition."

Baby sighed and shook her head, but she stood. She gave Rex the front view and the back, still holding the magazine. "Happy?" She dropped back into the tub, the water bubbling at her chin.

"Just the way I remembered it from so long ago." Rex walked to the edge of the tub, behind Baby. He knelt, reached over her shoulder, and took the *Soap Opera Digest* out of her hand. "Hey," she said.

"Wasn't sure I'd even find you here," Rex said. "Just the other day somebody ast me, The hell does your wife do all day? I had to answer him, You know, I have no idea. Made me feel kinda silly, tell you the truth."

Baby faced straight ahead. "Have you looked at the house lately, Rex? Did you notice the new dining room chairs? Did you see the new pillows in the den? How about the new cage for the parakeet?"

"Sure, I seen 'em."

"No, you didn't. All the work I'm doing to fix things up and you don't appreciate any of it. You come home at four in the morning, you sleep four or five hours, and then it's so long again till four in the morning. So what if I'm finding us some nice things, you don't give a crap. So what if I'm—"

"I got a business to run."

"—spending all my time and energy in furniture stores, what's the difference, you don't care."

Rex leaned close to Baby's ear. "You're spendin' all your time in stores? That's not what I hear."

"You think it's easy. I don't get no credit at all for what I'm trying to do for you. All you want to—"

"Heard you was in Baggett yesterday," Rex said.

He listened to the sound of the pump and the bubbling water. He could have counted to three or four by the time Baby said, "So?"

"Why was that?" Rex said.

"I go out there and swim sometimes. I told you that."

"Heard that squirrel from the inshurnce company was out there talkin' to you."

Baby started to stand. Rex put his left hand on her shoulder and pushed her back down. "Just stay where you are."

"Who told you all this?"

Rex began to stroke her hair with his right hand. "What did he wanna know?"

"He just said there was an insurance policy from when Mingo drowned, that's all, asking me if I knew anything about what happened."

Now Rex ran his fingers through Baby's hair, starting just behind her ear and moving slowly to her shoulder blades, careful not to pull hard when he hit a tangle. "What did you tell him?"

"I didn't tell him anything, Rex. Except to get lost, I told him that."

"Then how come he was out to the house for over an hour?"

Baby tried to turn but Rex gripped her shoulder. "Who said that? That insurance guy? If he told you that Rex, he's lying." She pushed at her collarbone, trying to pry his fingers from her shoulder. "You're hurting me," she said.

"Somebody's lyin', all right. And I got a good idea who." He closed his hand around her hair, thick as a dock rope in his grasp.

"Rex," she said. "I'm telling you the—"

He pushed down. Whatever else she had to say was coming up with the bubbles now. Rex sang.

> Sure, I still think of her time and again.
> The way that I see it, that ain't no big sin.
> Don't worry at night if I call out her name.
> She don't light my fire, she's just an old flame.

He pulled up on the hair. Baby came out of the water coughing, sucking air, and coughing some more. Rex leaned over to look into her eyes. "Lemme ask you again," he said. "What did you tell this man from the inshurnce company?"

"Nothing," she said. Her chest was heaving. "I swear to God. I didn't—"

This time she had braced her hands on the bottom of the tub and her feet against the other end, so he had to push harder to get her under.

"The second verse," Rex said, "goes a little like this."

Sometimes old memories will wander around.
Just like stray dogs that escape from the pound.
That don't mean her picture is back in the frame.
She once scorched my heart, but she's just an old flame.

Rex pulled her up again, let her cough some more and spit up some water. He released her hair and she lurched to the other side of the tub.

"What did you tell him?" he said.

"I told you already." She had draped herself over the edge of the tub, her forearms flat on the deck, her head lying on her forearms.

Rex waited for her to stop coughing. "Who'd he wanna know about?"

"Mingo, that's all. He asked about Mingo. I told him I barely knew Mingo."

Rex stood. "What else?"

"There wasn't nothing else."

He circled the tub and stopped with his boots a few inches from her head. She was shaking. "Bad enough that we already had one person drownded," Rex said. "Here's my advice. Next time that squirrel tries to talk to you, think . . . " He knelt again and grabbed a handful of hair once more. Baby stiffened.

"Think," Rex said, "how sad it'd be if we had somebody else go into the water and not come back out."

20 "Don't get the idea it was just Hackett," Tony said. "No way. Plenty of stars saluted when the name Tony Angel Productions was mentioned."

He turned off the van's radio. They were parked in the school lot, watching the house at 3585 Normandy. "Hey, one time Telly Savalas gave me a big hug. You believe that? I thought he was gonna kiss me. That Telly."

Mitch put his lighter away. "Who loves ya, baby?"

"Telly knew he was dealing with talent, he saw Tony Angel. There's a code in the business, Mitch. A pro respects a pro. I went up to Telly's suite for a promotional shoot, he says, Whatever you want, Tony, whatever you need, just say the word."

Mitch said, "I guess this was, like, before he died."

Tony turned to Mitch. "The fuck are you talking about?"

"The guy that was Kojak?" Mitch rubbed his scalp. "Too bad he croaked, huh?"

"That's not funny, Mitch."

"No, man, I saw it on TV."

Tony pointed, his finger just under Mitch's nose ring. "Don't you ever, ever, fuck with me like that. You hear me, Mitch? You think you're making a funny joke? You see me laughing? No, you don't. Telly's a friend of mine, and your sense of humor is burning my ass. You got that?"

"I was just trying to tell you what I—"

"I said, you got that?"

Mitch sighed. "I got it."

"Good. You got it, finally, it's about frigging time. One thing you'll have to learn, Mitch, you stay in this business long enough, is how to act. And I'll tell you how: You watch the stars. The stars are experts on how to dress, how to talk, how to *act*, Mitch. Watch the stars, because stars teach you class. They teach you how to dress class, how to talk class, and—uh-oh, here comes the jerkoff." The door opened at the upstairs apartment across the street. "You ready, Mitch? Don't go mental on me and blow it."

"I'm ain't gonna blow it." Mitch raised the video camera and pointed it through the van's windshield. "Tape's rolling," he said.

"Check it out, he has a babe with him."

"They're both in the frame."

"All right," Tony said. "All right, keep it on them when they come down the stairs. Make sure you got some of the dashboard in the foreground. I want that surveillance look, you understand? The whole look has got to be ... right there."

"You told me that already," Mitch said.

"Now, I want you to zoom in and out of focus a couple of times real quick to give it, you know, the right tone."

"You told me that, too."

"All right," Tony said, "stay with them across the yard, stay with them, here they come."

"In the crosshairs."

Tony clapped his hands softly. "This frigging loser'll never know what hit him. Fuck with Tony Angel, see what happens, asshole ... Now when he goes to his truck, Mitch, you stay with the babe, let's see where she ends up."

"I'm on the case." Mitch kept the camera on the woman as she walked around the truck and opened the passenger door. "She's going with him."

"Hey, I can see," Tony said. "The eyes are working today. Keep it rolling, Mitch, we'll follow the truck. Every move he makes, we'll have the camera on him. He goes to take a leak, we'll be watching. The frigging jerk. All right, here we go." Tony pushed the gas pedal in halfway and turned the ignition key. The van's engine answered with a couple of syrupy, low-power half-cranks.

The blue truck pulled away from the curb and rolled down the street away from them. "Come on, you fucking hunka junk." Tony turned the van's key again and got only a feeble click.

He pounded the steering wheel. "Shit!"

Mitch lowered the camera. "Sorry, man," he said. "I was thinking I should get, like, a new battery."

"You don't mind, do you?" Sally said. "I haven't eaten since yesterday afternoon."

Jack drove the truck down Normandy, away from the house. "What do you feel like?"

"You pick. I just needed to get out for a while."

They drove in silence for several blocks, Jack heading

east now on Mockingbird Lane. "This is not bad, the sunshine," Sally said as they passed over North Central Expressway. "You work in a bar, you don't see much sun. See a lot of other things, though." She turned to him. "How'd you find me? I'm not in the phone book."

"Driver's license records." Jack went right on Greenville Avenue, then pulled an index card from his shirt pocket. He read what he had written. "Sally Ann Danvers, 3585 Normandy, five-nine, one-hundred-twenty-three pounds. Age, let's see, twenty-six." He smiled.

"The thing about you? I have this feeling you've been watching me."

Jack changed the subject. "If you like seafood this is a good place." He steered into the parking lot of a small restaurant that could pass for a shack on the beach.

"Strange, when I woke up today," Sally said, "I saw someone leaving my room. At first I thought it was April, but I don't think so anymore."

Jack switched the ignition off and faced her, expecting angry eyes but not finding them. She said, "Was that you?"

"It's not what you're thinking."

"How do you know what I'm thinking?"

"The apartment door was open. I knocked, I called out. Nobody answered. I thought something bad might have happened. I walked in and there you were."

She raised her chin. "What did you do then?"

Jack looked at his feet, then came back to her. "I watched you sleep."

"Watched me sleep." She started to smile but seemed to decide not to. "What else were you doing?"

Jack wasn't sure if he should say it but the words tumbled out before he could throw up the gates. "Wishing I was there in bed with you."

Sally looked away. Jack watched her pull the door handle and step from the truck. Before she shut the door she leaned back into the cab. "That might have been fun," she said.

They sat at a picnic table on a porch that had been enclosed with clear plastic sheeting for the winter. Both ate boiled shrimp from paper plates. Sally sipped from a mug of beer that left a foam mustache on her lip. She licked it off and said, "To get to my story."

"Right."

"I'll give you the quick version. You already know where I grew up. My dad's a plumber. I came up to Dallas to go to school. Senior year, I met a guy named Steve. We went out for six months and then we got married. That was my first mistake."

Jack nodded. "Lots of people make that one."

"Steve liked to drink and run around, but not with me ... I was a dancer in school. So I stayed in shape, right? You know what Steve told me? He'd decided he liked plump girls."

Jack watched her light a cigarette. She had long, thin hands that moved quickly. "We split last year. I wasn't much in the mood for anything after that. I had a friend who liked to do a little cocaine, so I started doing a little with her, and then I started doing a lot. For a month or two or five, I guess, I don't know. I dropped into the hole. Some days that was the only reason I had for getting out of bed." Sally seemed to be thinking about it, then asked, "You ever do coke?"

Jack shook his head. "That was my big brother's game for a while."

"He stopped?"

"He had to. It killed him."

"What did you do?"

"What did I do? I spoke at his funeral and I helped carry his coffin out of the church. After that I went to my mother's house a lot of nights and listened to her cry and ask why it had happened. What can you say? It happened because he did too much coke."

Sally reached across the table and touched his arm. "I'm sorry."

"It was a long time ago."

"Lucky for me I got some help. Bobby Slater."

"Hey, Bobby," Jack said. "I almost forgot we were supposed to be talking about Bobby."

"Funny thing is, he was my ex-husband's friend. One day he comes by, just out of the blue. I guess he found me in pretty bad shape, 'cause he looked at me and he said, You're coming with me."

"And you went."

"To Guymon, Oklahoma."

Jack peeled a shrimp. "I'll have to get out the Rand McNally for that one."

"It's like you're driving to the end of the earth. You wonder if you'll see another tree again. But I'll tell you, I didn't care where we were going or what we were doing. I didn't care."

"I've known that feeling."

"We finally pulled into Guymon and Bobby says, First you're going to my doctor and then I'm turning you over to my mother. The doctor gave me vitamins and antibiotics and his mom let me have a place to stay."

Jack sat at the table, watching the way Sally moved and listening to her talk. Seeing himself as a masted ship too long in the doldrums with a scurvied crew near mutiny, but with its sails filling at last. The kind of vision you could have in a restaurant where the counter help wore yachting caps.

"I spent the summer up there," she said. "Mrs. Slater and I watched soap operas together and baked a lot of pies. Bobby visited every other weekend. Sundays we took his mom to the Guymon Bible Church, and let me tell you, that's some serious Jesus action there."

"Be right back." Jack got two more beers and returned to the table.

"So," Sally said, "in September I came back to Dallas. I rented an apartment, and Bobby got me the job at the Melon Patch. End of story. Happy now?"

Jack watched her watch the traffic on Greenville.

"I think Bobby saved my life," she said after a while. "The way he found me and picked me up, I'm sure he did." She paused and took a breath. "I have this feeling that right now he needs me to do the same thing for him."

She turned the bleached blue eyes on Jack and said, "Let's go find him."

There was no car in the driveway next door. "We must be living right," Jack said, easing his truck to the curb in front of Bobby Slater's house on McGraw Street. "Looks like the owner's not around. We'd have to do some fast-talking and two-stepping, he was here."

Jack stared toward Bobby's porch. The mailbox where he had found Sally's postcard from Galveston was not overflowing this time. The curtains were still closed, but he saw no unclaimed newspapers in the front yard. "When's the last time you talked to Bobby's mother?" he said.

"What's today, Tuesday?" Sally seemed to think it over. "Sunday night."

"What did she say?"

"She said she hadn't heard from him in several weeks."

"Several as in what—three or four? That puts it right about the time Mingo No-Bird turned up dead. You think it's really been that long?" Jack switched off the ignition. "Let's sit here for a minute before we go barging in. Make sure there's no big dogs or bad dudes hanging."

"Listen," Sally said. "Are you listening?"

Jack kept his gaze on the house. "Every word."

"Before we do this, I want to be sure you understand me. Bobby's a really nice guy. He's not the type."

"He's not what type?"

"The type to do something against the law. To do it and then run off and hide. That's what you've been thinking all along, isn't it? That this whole deal has something wrong with it, and Bobby's part of it, so he's hiding somewhere?"

Jack shifted to face her. "It was a simple question."

She shook her head, looking confused or irritated, he wasn't sure which. "What was a simple question?"

He watched the house again. "When she said three or four weeks . . . you think Bobby's mother was telling you the truth?"

Sally voice grew louder. "No, see, I think this nice silver-haired lady in Guymon, Oklahoma, who spends all day making pies, is in on some big crime with her son. So when I call, even though I'm their friend, she thinks I'm an FBI agent and she covers everything up. Screw you."

When she was finished Jack turned to look. She had the sharp nod of somebody who wanted to punch him in the mouth. He said, "Just asking."

"This woman, you know what she does at night? She listens to Jim Nabors records."

"It's the lawyer in me. It's like malaria. You think you're well for a while but the fever keeps coming back."

"Jim Nabors, every night before bed," Sally said. "She sings along to them. 'Oh My Papa,' that's her favorite."

Jack studied the house some more. "Bobby and Baby," he said, his breath fogging the window. "Baby and Bobby, that's a cute one. Kinda sounds like a lounge act of its own. How long have they been carrying on?"

"I don't know," Sally said. "Six months maybe. I only talked to Bobby about it a couple of times. It's not something he wanted everybody to know about."

"You're jumping the boss's wife, you don't broadcast it around the workplace. Hard to make vice president that way."

"I told him to break it off. I told him plenty of times, this is a really stupid thing you're doing."

"And did he listen? Of course not. They never do." Jack turned to her, watching her eyes go over his face. He said, "The stories I could tell."

"Go ahead."

"Not today."

She waited awhile, then said, "Bobby told me Baby was in love with him. He was worried if he cut her off she'd do something crazy."

"You're saying he thought she was a little nuts."

"I think she was a lot nuts, the way Bobby used to talk."

"So he taught her how to shoot a handgun?" Jack wagged his head. "Some people know how to keep life interesting."

They sat in the truck cab another ten minutes. A couple of cars went past them and drove on. Some children played in the front yard three houses down. Sally smoked a cigarette. A blanket of high, flat clouds had moved in, making the afternoon sun look like a bare bulb shining through wax paper.

Jack said, "Well, let's get this done before the owner comes home."

They got out of the truck and walked across the brown yard together. Sally said, "I feel funny doing this."

Jack took her elbow as they mounted the steps to the porch. "Hey, we're not going in to boost his VCR. Don't worry, you're not a big-time lawbreaker doing something bad here."

She pulled away from his grip and squared around, blocking his path to the door. "I don't care about *bad*, all right? I don't even care about the law."

Jack glanced toward the street. "You know, fighting here on the front porch might not be the stealthiest way to break into a house."

She didn't get any quieter. "I care about my friend. That's what I care about, that's all I care about right now."

"Okay, fine." Jack took a deep breath and put his hands out, touching the air around her shoulders. "You've made yourself clear."

She said, "Boy, you piss me off with your little lectures."

"Like I'm the only one with the lectures." Jack dropped his hands. "That's all I've been getting from you since we got here."

"What do you expect with the way—"

"All I've had is you telling me what a bag of slime I am because I ask some questions, like I'm not supposed to ask anything unless it's polite—"

"—just because you think everybody's dirty, and maybe the people you know are. But you know what? It's not everybody."

"So I'm just supposed to shut up," Jack said, "and make nice because it might hurt somebody's feelings, like yours or your friends'?"

"What do you know about friends?"

"—even though one of these friends of yours might be up to his ass in trouble, and maybe by asking these questions you don't like, maybe I'm helping him out."

They were close enough that he could feel her breath on him. If he leaned in any farther they would be touching. Someone watching them might think they were about to kiss now that they had stopped shouting. Jack thought of her in the bed again and had to turn away, trying to get his head back to business.

When he turned he saw a large woman in the yard across the street. She stood at her curb in an overcoat with a nightgown peaking out from the bottom. Her arms were folded as she beamed in on Sally and Jack. "Great," Jack said. "Probably the neighborhood crime watch. As soon as we're in the house she's on the phone to the cops." He waved. She didn't wave back. "Well, we're screwed now. So much for this big strategy, thank you very much."

"I'll take care of this." Sally brushed past him, and walked through the yard and across the street. Jack watched the two women talk. In a couple of minutes Sally was back. "Her name's Louise," Sally said. "She's been in the hospital. Every day she's supposed to get out of the house and walk to the curb and back, doctor's orders."

"And who does she suspect we are?"

"I told her I was Bobby's sister."

Jack nodded. "Has she seen Bobby lately?"

"Did you hear me? I said she's been in the hospital." Sally looked at the door. "Are we doing this or not?"

"Yeah, we're doing it." Jack leaned against the doorframe and reached to his back pocket for a pair of vise grips he had brought from the truck. "All right, here's the deal. We'll look for any signs that Bobby's been here the last few days—fresh garbage, recent newspapers, that kind of thing. If you see an address book, grab it. If you see a phone bill, grab that, too. That'll let us know who he's been calling long-distance. I'll try to find where he keeps his bills, see if we can pick up some credit card numbers."

Jack tapped the casing of the deadbolt lock with the vise grips. "Doesn't look like Fort Knox here. Shouldn't take long to get this thing off."

"Before you start with that," she said from behind him. With Jack thinking, Jesus, now what? "Before you start tearing the lock apart," she said, "why don't you check to see if the door's open?"

Jack closed his eyes for a couple of seconds. "All right," he said. "If you want." He turned the knob and gave a slight push. It was unlocked.

He held the door barely open, just touching the frame, and looked over his shoulder at Sally. "One other thing. Check in his closet and see if a lot of clothes are gone. Like maybe he packed for a long trip."

"I already thought of that."

"Okay," he said, ready to give the door a push but not

doing it. "I'll go in first and I'll let you know when it's all right to follow." What he didn't tell her was that it wouldn't surprise him, not really, to walk in and find Bobby's body inside. To walk in and discover Bobby on the floor beside a pool of congealed blood from the hole in his head or the slash in his neck. Or hanging from a light fixture by a necktie noose.

He looked back at Sally once more, but before he could speak she said, "Oh, come on," and reached past him to give the door a shove.

The sound of it told him all he needed to know—the squeak of the hinges and then the bang of the doorknob hitting the wall. It was too hard, had too much echo, the kind of sound that bounces off walls with no pictures and floors with no rugs.

He stepped inside the darkened room with Sally right behind him. "I can't believe this," she said.

Like the sound from the door, her words had the slightest echo, coming back to them off the bare sheetrock and wood. The house was empty.

They only had to wait fifteen or twenty minutes for the owner to pull into the driveway next door in an El Camino with squeaky shocks. He was wearing the same dirty jumpsuit and sour face as last time Jack had talked to him.

"Hey, remember me?" Jack said as the man stepped from his car. "I came around looking for Bobby Slater the other day."

"He ain't here," the man said. He was carrying a twelve-pack of Busch Bavarian and a carton of Winstons.

"I see that. In fact, I see that he moved out." The man glared but didn't answer. "When did he move? And did he tell you where he was going?"

The man spat through his teeth onto his driveway. "Think I tole you last time. I don't poke around in my tenants' stuff."

Jack started to ask another question but Sally, standing next to him, cut him off. "Do you own this place?" she asked the man.

He gave Sally a long, uncertain look before answering, "Yeah?"

Jack said to Sally, "What's that got to do with—"

"Give me a chance," she said to him, putting a hand on his arm. Then, to the man, "We were just in the house over there and I noticed you've got copper pipes carrying the gas to the water heater."

The man waited even longer. "Yeah?"

"Well," Sally said, "you have to know that won't pass city code. I mean, if I got the housing inspectors out here they'd be all over you like a cheap, uh, you know—"

"Suit," Jack said.

"All over you like a suit about that. They'd probably want to take a good look at the wiring, too. I can see you having to spend a lot of money to fix all this up just so you can rent the place again. That'd be a shame, wouldn't it?"

Jack watched him, the way he sagged, blew out some air, and gazed into the distance. He saw a guy who must ask the question every day before he walked out of the house, Who's busting my balls today? The man said, "What the hell is it you want, lady?"

"Where's Bobby Slater?" Sally said.

"I ain't seen him for three, four weeks."

"When did he move out?" she asked.

"He didn't move out. His brother come the day before yesterday with a crew and took all his stuff."

Jack looked at Sally and said, "Brother?" She shook her head no.

"Paid off the rest of Bobby's lease," the man said. "In cash, all six months of it."

"What's this brother's name?" Jack asked.

"Hell, I don't know," the man said. "Short dude with a cowboy hat and sunglasses, 'sall I can tell you. Stood right where you're standin' while some Mexicans loaded up the truck. Kept wantin' me to listen to him sing stupid songs he said he wrote."

Loyce Slapp sat on the couch in Rex Echols's office, going through the brochures he had picked up at a travel agency that morning. He had some from Barbados, the Bahamas, the Virgin Islands, and a place he'd never heard of, Martinique. The pictures could break your heart—water so clear, sand so white, couples arm in arm at sunset. He couldn't wait to show them to April. Tell her, That's where we'll be, I promise, in those slatted wooden chairs beneath that same palm tree, you and me, soon.

April wasn't due at the Melon Patch Ranch for another half-hour, so Loyce waited. Wondering what it would be like, just getting to the islands, flying in an airplane over that much water. The only time Loyce had been on a jet, he went to a county sheriffs' convention in Atlanta. He could imagine looking out the window of the plane and seeing nothing but blue sky and ocean as he passed over to his new life.

He stood, stretched, and rubbed his eyes. It hadn't

been the best of nights. No sleep, then the screwup with the insurance investigator at the Heart-o-the-Pines Lodge. Afterward, driving away from the motel, Loyce had a flash of panic. For a bad moment he could see everything falling apart, leaving him with no money, no April, and no escape, leaving him as nothing but sheriff in Baggett County—if that.

That morning, after the problems at the Heart-o-the-Pines, he had gone back home. But Loyce stayed in his driveway, in the cold and darkness before dawn, unable to make himself get out of the patrol car. He couldn't go into the house. It had two bedrooms and one bath with twenty-three years of payments left, a brown brick exterior with chocolate brown trim that needed paint, a roof going bad, termites that the exterminator wanted $400 to kill, bird-shit-green carpet ruined by two worthless dogs, a wife asleep in her recliner with the TV going and Pop-Tart crumbs on her chest. A wife who had put on forty or fifty pounds in the seventeen years they had been married, and with no pregnancy to blame. Who spent a lot of time reading *Guideposts* magazine and watching the *700 Club*. Every time someone on the show prayed, she closed her eyes and lifted her hands above her head. When the people on television spoke in tongues, so did Loyce's wife. She was forty-five years old and was losing her goddamn hair.

After fifteen minutes of sitting in front of his house, he had shifted the car into reverse, backed out, and headed to Dallas. As he drove he slipped his hand into his right front pocket. Running his fingers over a single key there, dreaming: An envelope arrives on the desk of the Baggett County clerk. It's postmarked from an island in the

Caribbean. The clerk opens the envelope and the key that's now in his pocket falls out, along with Sheriff Loyce Slapp's one-page letter of instruction.

Take the key to the Baggett State Bank, the letter says. It will open a safe deposit box there. Inside the safe deposit box you will find my letter of resignation as sheriff, along with written instructions to my lawyer to begin immediate divorce proceedings.

The drive had calmed him some. He would go to Dallas and see Rex Echols, make sure everything was still screwed down tight. Make sure Rex wasn't busy singing songs while the wheels fell off.

As he came closer to the city the billboards had started, the ones with the girls in bikinis, selling beer and cigarettes. There was one for Coors, especially—a blonde in a red bathing suit. The thighs she had. It used to make him crazy, looking at those girls, until he got one of his own.

"I do believe I took care of it," Rex said as he walked into his office at the Melon Patch. "I'd say it's handled. I think it's safe to say Baby Echols'll think three or four times before she blabs anything else to that damn squirrel."

"What has she told him already?" Loyce Slapp said from the couch. "How much did she hurt us yesterday?"

Rex sat in his chair, leaned back, and propped his boots on his desk. "I ast her that very question, Sheriff. Used a kinda truth serum on her, you might call it. I don't think she told him a thing. If she did, we'll find out."

156

Loyce shook his head. "I don't want this left to chance."

"That's why I went out right away," Rex said. "That's why I dropped everthing I was doin' and took care of bidness . . . She was surprised as hell that I knew about it, tell you what. I don't think she's ever figured out that you've been watchin'."

Loyce nodded. "I'm careful to stay on down the highway a couple of miles away. We've got a little clearing behind some bushes that we use for radar work, and I park there. Lets me know who's coming and going. But I keep my distance."

"Except for once or twice," Rex said with a wink. "Those times you went crawlin' through the woods."

Loyce sniffed. "We had to make the case."

Rex stood, then bent over a file cabinet behind his desk, searching through the papers in an open drawer. "Here's the skinny." He displayed a red folder. "Here's what got the whole ball rollin'."

Loyce went over his teeth with his tongue, wondering why Rex would want to pull out the reports again. Rex opened the folder on his desk and shuffled through some typewritten pages. "This is it," Rex said, tapping his finger on one sheet. "Let's see, where's the good part . . . here we go." He began to read out loud, "Officer approached the rear of house on foot, hidden by brush. Officer observed subject Barbara Echols and subject Robert Slater emerge from pool. Both subjects were nude. Officer then observed subjects engage in apparent sexual intercourse on furniture adjacent to pool."

Rex tossed the paper down and slapped the file shut. Loyce watched his color change, heard his breathing pick up. "One thing I never ast," Rex said. "One thing. When these two are goin' at it, who's on top?"

"On top?" Loyce said. Thinking Rex was just like the dumb ones he arrested every now and then who almost begged for a beating. "Your wife was."

Rex tightened. He mashed one hand against his face. "What else?" he said. "Go ahead, pour it on."

Loyce thought about ending the show, but it was too much fun. "Your wife was howling to wake the dead."

The veins bulged on Rex's neck. He gave slow vent to a breath. "When this is all over, I'm gonna take care of her. You wait and see. I'll take the wheels off her wagon."

Loyce glanced at his watch. April should be arriving any time. He picked up his brochures and stood.

"Gonna take care of lots of people when this is over," Rex said.

"I'm leaving," Loyce said. "After I talk to April, I have to get back to Baggett."

"That's right." Rex seemed to calm himself down. He leaned back in his chair again. "Y'all had a crime wave last night, didn't you? Shit. I still don't understand how the hell this happened. I mean, how hard can it be?"

Loyce looked at the ceiling, then at Rex. "I told you. He changed rooms on us."

"Un-damn-believable ... And how was our *hit*man this mornin', anyway? How was Mister Robert Slater? That's what I call him now. He feelin' all right?"

"He has a headache. That chair that was broken across his face tore him up pretty good."

"Poor baby." Rex's feet went on his desktop again. "He was the wrong man for that job. I coulda tole you that."

Loyce swallowed hard, trying to keep his irritation down. "What was I supposed to do, recruit somebody from town? Somebody who'd have told everybody in Baggett what happened?"

"I know, I know." Rex held up his hands. "We shoulda just had him use a gun. That way you don't leave so much to chance."

"That way," Loyce said, "everybody within a quarter-mile knows something's going down."

Rex sighed. "Well, it's done . . . I hope you said to him, I hope you tole Mister Robert Slater to get his butt back to his safe house and stay there."

"That's where I left him at four-thirty this morning. Lying on the bed with an icepack on his forehead."

"Think we oughta move him somewhere else? Think it's okay for him to be where he is?"

Loyce wondered how many times he would have to explain this to Rex. They were using a lake cabin that belonged to the owner of a Houston Toyota dealership. No neighbors, with thick woods around it, but it had heat, phone, and a satellite dish for the TV. Loyce would have traded it for his own house in an instant. "Look," Loyce said, "the owner calls me himself, personally, whenever anybody is coming up to use that cabin. He checks in with the sheriff. Nobody ever arrives unannounced."

"If you say so." Rex pulled his boots from his desk and stood. "You headed back to Baggett? I got somethin' for you to take." He disappeared under his desk and came back out with a shoebox. "Here you go."

Loyce stepped forward to take it.

"It's all the important papers I could find when we moved his stuff outta that old house," Rex said. "I think they's a birth certificate in there, a Social Security card, maybe even a passport. Everthing a Mister Robert Slater needs to start his brand new life somewhere else."

23 Cactus Bloodworth's office occupied a quarter of the ninth floor of a blue-green mirrored box on North Central Expressway. He had furnished it with mounted steer horns, paintings of Indians, buffalo statuettes, and a couple of bearskin rugs. In one corner was a fake Christmas tree draped with a string of lights shaped like jalapeño peppers. Cactus himself was wearing a bolo tie with his Armani suit. He said, "I'm damn glad you came by, Jack, you and your lovely friend here, 'cause I was just about to call you."

Jack and Sally sat in leather-upholstered chairs facing Cactus's desk. They had come straight from what had been Bobby Slater's house. "Things have been heating up on that Baggett County case," Jack said. "Knock on any wall and you hear rats scurrying on the other side."

"You ever been to Ha-wah-yah?" Cactus was looking at Sally.

"Supposed to be nice," she said.

"Beautiful place. Beautiful." Cactus stroked his silver mustache. Behind him the view was of a freeway, shopping centers, and apartment complexes. "You're laying on one of those beaches in that sun, life's pretty much worth living. Tell you what, you do that for a few days and it's hard to come on home and put the nose back to the grindstone."

Sally smiled. "That's what I've always heard."

"Old Cactus comes back here"—he waved at the room—"and the paperwork's all backed up. Takes two or three days just to get up to speed. Pretty soon all that relaxation you pick up on the beach, it's all gone."

Jack said, "Sally works for the policyholder on this case out of Baggett County."

"Got married over there, you know." Cactus was still looking at Sally. "Right there on the beach, in our bathing suits, me and Nikki."

"Congratulations," Sally said.

"Right at sundown, our bare feet in the sand, me and Nikki. Flame lanterns on bamboo sticks flickering all around us. The hotel had a band playing for happy hour out by the pool. Know what they did? Stopped what they were doing and played 'Here Comes the Bride' for us, Hawah-yan style."

"That sounds great," Sally said.

"The hotel had another surprise for us. Right after we said our I-do's they wheel us out a feast. Big table full a food, and what do you think is right smack in the middle of it? What do you think the centerpiece is? Take a wild guess. It's one a those barbecued pigs with an apple stuck in its mouth." Cactus shook his head. "I thought Nikki was never gonna stop screaming."

Jack said, "We've got a missing—"

"She's crying and yelling, 'God, that's disgusting!' and 'Get me away from these animal killers!' The poor waiters are standing there in white jackets, and Nikki's screaming that they're all pig murderers. Took me better than two hours to get her calmed down. Boy oh boy."

Jack waited until he was sure Cactus had finished his story. "There's a missing witness in this case, Cactus, and everywhere you poke your finger, you find rot. Top to bottom."

Cactus winked at Sally. "Old Jack's a good man. Give him a job and he goes after it. That's what I like about him."

She glanced at Jack. "I know what you mean."

"Jumps right in the water, even if there's sharks. Right, Jack? Hell, especially if there's sharks. No fun without the sharks."

"Tell me why I get the feeling," Jack said, "that you're not all that hot to talk about this case I'm working."

Cactus ran a hand through the Buffalo Bill hair. "Like I said, Jack, the paperwork was all stacked up when I got back to town. So I didn't find some things until this afternoon. I was about to call you. Here's why."

He stretched across the desk to hand Jack a sheet of paper. It had a slippery feel and was slightly curled, a fax transmission. The letterhead, in bold block letters, said Continental Centurion Associates. Beneath that, in smaller script, was Office of Claims Investigations.

Cactus said, "Came late yesterday, I believe."

Jack read the letter, three short paragraphs, and passed it to Sally. "A lot has happened since they wrote that," he said. "Enough to change their mind, believe me."

"Jack, Jack," Cactus said.

"This sucks," Sally said. She leaned forward and put the letter on Cactus's desk.

"This is a big mistake," Jack said. "It's crazy."

"Well, you two are ganging up on old Cactus now." He picked up the letter, held it at full arm's length and read out loud. "In the matter of Rex T. Echols, policy number et cetera, et cetera . . . Due to the information contained in official law enforcement findings, this office has determined not to pursue further investigation . . . Will recommend that the insured be paid in full . . . Recommendation to be forwarded to office of vice president for policyholder services and claims adjustment." He looked up from the paper. "Seems pretty clear to old Cactus. What is it you two don't understand?"

"Call them," Jack said. "Tell them there's new evidence. You can do that. They know you."

Cactus squinted and tugged at his earlobe. "Look at it from their viewpoint, Jack." He held up another sheet. "It's in your own report to them. The sheriff says it was an accidental drowning. The justice of the peace says the same thing."

Jack pointed. "Look at the rest of my report, Cactus. Look at the stuff about the sheriff's sloppy investigation and the missing evidence and the witness who hasn't been seen since."

"Come on, he's disappeared," Sally said. "That ought to count for something. Even to some limps at an insurance company."

Cactus tossed the paper back onto his desk. "What's the company supposed to do, Jack? Refuse to pay? They do that, they'll end up in court. In Baggett County, no less. Telling a jury full a home folks that they can't prove it, but they think their duly elected officials are a bunch of liars and fraud artists. They'll get hammered. They'll get punitive damages from here to Confederate Heroes Day."

Jack shook his head. "Who says Baggett County has to be the venue?"

"Who says it won't? This dude with the policy, whatever his name—"

"Rex Echols," Sally and Jack said.

"This dude can file wherever he damn pleases. Come on, you know all this."

"Ask the company to wait a while," Jack said. "Tell them we need a couple more weeks."

"Good money after bad, Jack, as far as they're concerned. Why should they want to run up more gumshoe fees when they've already decided they're gonna have to pay out on the policy?"

Sally asked, "Why does it have to be just about money?"

Cactus smoothed his mustache, cleared his throat, and folded his hands on the desk in front of him. "And just what else, darling, is it supposed to be about?"

She turned to Jack. "Do you think Rex knows yet?"

"I doubt it," he said.

Cactus gathered his papers into a stack. "Oh, it'll take the company weeks, maybe months, to get out the rubber stamp, put the final approval on it. But believe old Cactus, folks, it's as good as a done deal."

"It doesn't have to be," Jack said. He and Sally looked at each other.

Cactus read from the letter again. "It says here, 'This office has determined not to pursue any further investigation.'" He handed the letter back to Jack. "Let me translate that for you, Jackie. It means they ain't paying us any more money. So as far as old Cactus is concerned, this case is closed."

24 The sheriff finished his beer and belched. Rex Echols did a double-take. He said, "Sheriff, I don't believe I've ever heard you burp in public before. Tell you what, standards are droppin' all over the place."

Loyce Slapp sat on a barstool at the Melon Patch Ranch, watching April Showers wait tables. Rex had already asked him a couple of times if he shouldn't head on home to East Texas. Now Rex said, "Hope nobody's robbin' the bank in Baggett today." He was grinning but with a needle, Loyce could tell.

"How many's he had?" Rex asked a waitress, who answered with one hand, fingers splayed. "Five? *Five*?" Rex turned his dark glasses toward Loyce. "Since when do you drink more than one or two?"

Loyce stared back. "Since whenever I want to."

"Hope they ain't no shopliftin' down at the Baggett five-and-dime this afternoon."

"You're so worried about it, you go check," Loyce said. "I don't feel like it."

He had planned to leave two hours earlier, after giving the travel brochures to April. "Cool," she had said when he showed her the photos of boats and beaches. Then she kissed him, hard. He couldn't make himself walk out the door after that.

"You're so damn worried about Baggett?" Loyce said to Rex. "Here's my keys. You go check." Thinking, *You* go work in that nowhere town. *You* go live in that shitty little house with a fat woman who prays all the time, see how long you last. Loyce signaled for beer number six.

He watched April cross the room with a trayful of drinks. "The way she walks," Loyce said, "you couldn't imagine it any better." He turned back to the bar to tell that to Rex, but Rex was gone.

He got his sixth beer. Loyce had a gulp, and another, and moved around on his stool so he could marvel at April some more. She was serving a table of three. Young guys in jeans and T-shirts. April set three glasses on the table, and they all stared at April's tits when she bent over. You can't blame them for that, seemed to Loyce. It would take a dead man not to look.

But then one of them touched the outside of her thigh. He moved up and kept on going. If he didn't stop he would run his hand inside her shorts.

Loyce came off his stool. He saw April try to twist away. The man had his other arm around her, gripping her hip. He was laughing when Loyce reached the table. Loyce stood with his hands at his side and said, "Let her go."

"Huh?" The man said turned to his friends. "What'd he say?" Then back to Loyce, "I don't read lips, dude."

April said, "It's okay, Loyce."

"Let her go," Loyce said louder.

"The lady doesn't seem to mind," the man said. "She seems to like it." He had a face like some of the big-city college boys Loyce would pull over on the highway every now and then, the ones who thought they were smarter than everybody else until Loyce handled them.

Fingers went to the inside of April's thigh. Loyce put his hand under his coat and came back out with his .38. He had been too slow to pull it in the room at the Heart-o-the-Pines, but not this time. He raised it and pressed the barrel against the bridge of the man's nose, between his eyes. Thinking, Funny how fast a smile can disappear, how fast hands can drop away from a woman's leg.

"How much does he owe you?" Loyce asked April.

April checked her ticket. "Ten-fifty."

"Pay her," Loyce said. The man was cross-eyed, staring at the gun barrel. His friends were frozen. "Right now," Loyce said with a nudge of the gun. "Pay up." One of the friends came to life and produced a twenty. April made change, counting it out on the table a dollar at a time while Loyce kept the gun against the man's face. "There you go, hon," she said.

"What about a tip?" Loyce said. "She gives good service, doesn't she?" He moved the man's head up and down with the gun. "She deserves twenty percent, then. That's two dollars, plus."

Loyce took the bills and coins from the pile of change and handed them to April. "Thanks," April said, cheerful, looking right at the man with the gun to his head. "Y'all have a nice night, now."

"Meet me outside the front door," Loyce told her. When she had walked away Loyce pulled the gun from the man's face. "Touch any of the others you want," Loyce said, "but not her."

Darnell the bouncer had missed the whole thing. Loyce walked by him with a nod and found April out front, shivering. He took his coat off and draped it over her. "Let's get in my car," he said.

"You shouldn't have done what you did back there, Loyce."

He pointed. "Let's talk where it's warmer."

They slid into the front seat of the Baggett County patrol car. Loyce started the engine and turned the heater on high.

April said, "Loyce, baby, have you been drinkin' a little too much?"

"I don't want anybody else touching you. Just me and nobody else."

April laughed. "At the Melon Patch? How'm I supposed to get tips?"

Loyce raised a hand toward the building. "He would have put his hands right in your pants if I didn't stop him."

"He was just havin' fun," April said. She looked down at her chest and adjusted her spangled top so that a crescent of each nipple rose above the fabric.

"Listen." Loyce stroked the back of her neck. "We're going away together, right? You and me?"

"Sure," April opened the glove box and flipped up the makeup mirror. "Loyce, baby, is there a light in here?"

Loyce turned on the dome light. April checked her eye

makeup. "So just stop working now," Loyce said. "We'll be on a beach before you know it, soon as I get my money. What do you need to be working for?"

April took his hand from her neck, kissed it, and laid it on her breast. "You're cute," she said. "I better get back inside. Rex'll be real pissed if he finds out I'm gone."

Loyce snorted. "Big bad Rex."

"He will." April removed Loyce's hand from her breast and placed it on the seat beside her with a couple of pats. "He gets real mad if I take a break when I'm not supposed to. He always tells me"—she smiled—"the star has to be on-stage."

"Let me tell you about big bad Rex, okay? You should have seen him about an hour ago, the way I had him squirming. He didn't look like such a hot dog then."

"Give me a little kiss," April said. "I gotta go."

"You know what I've been doing? Watching Rex's wife make a damn fool of him. Big bad Rex, his wife's been screwing around on him for months."

April nodded. "I heard Baby had a little mischief going."

"She's out there in Baggett, screwing around on him with his own hired hand. Who's the sheriff in Baggett? Tell me that. Who's the sheriff?"

"You are, Loyce baby."

"Think I didn't know all about it? I documented it. I got it all down on paper. Every time Rex's wife got the hot beef—"

April giggled.

"—I made a report. Then I gave the reports to Rex. They're all over there in his office. He keeps them in a bright red folder. Ask him to give you a look. Ask him to read them out loud to you the way I made him do it for me. Big bad Rex."

"I better go." April leaned over and kissed him on the cheek. "Bye-bye."

"Hold on, I'll give you a ride back." Loyce shifted the car out of park.

"Loyce, I'm just going back inside the Melon Patch."

"I'll give you a police escort." Loyce took his foot off the brake and gave the car gas. It lurched backward and came to a hard stop with the sound of metal crunching.

They both got out. The left rear fender was crumpled around a three-inch pipe that was upright at the edge of the parking lot, sunk into the pavement and filled with concrete.

April hugged him. "Oh, baby, I'm so sorry."

Loyce looked at the mess. "Every time you have an accident in a county vehicle you have to fill out paperwork. Something like this, the county commissioners'll want to take it out of my pay."

April hugged him tighter. "Oh, no."

Loyce's hand went from her shoulder, down her back to her ass. "You think I care? You think Sheriff Loyce Slapp of Baggett County gives a shit? In a few weeks I'll be rich." He squeezed. "Rich and gone."

25 "He's going to get away with it, isn't he?" Sally cupped an ashtray in one hand and smoked her cigarette. "Whatever it is Rex did, he's got it made now."

"Except he doesn't know that," Jack said. Both of them stood behind Cactus Bloodworth's desk, looking out the window. The sky was dark but for an orange glow in the west, like a sheet of blue steel molten at one end.

Jack peered down at the crawl of suburban-bound traffic on North Central Expressway. Pink streetlights had blinked on. "Nobody's told Rex yet that he's got a winner." He pulled the folded letter from the insurance company out of his coat pocket, then stuck it back in. "Like Cactus said, it could be a while before he knows."

They were the only ones in the office. Cactus had told them to take their time, sit around and talk if they wanted, but he was late for an engagement. He had grabbed his black cowboy hat and his tooled-leather briefcase and left with, "Got to get you two out to the house for supper with me and Nikki sometime."

Sally gazed out the window and said, "So now what? You're off to your next case?"

Jack dropped into Cactus's chair. It was covered in soft black leather upholstery, more like an embrace than a place to sit. "Business is a little light right now. I've got a few odds and ends working, but nothing big."

Sally mashed her cigarette into the ashtray and put her forehead against the window glass. "Well, I'm going to keep looking for Bobby." She straightened and turned toward him. "That's what I'm going to do."

Jack looked her up and down and said, "I'm staying with it, too."

Sally stepped back and leaned against the desk, almost sitting on it, her arms folded. "What are you saying?"

"When somebody tries to bang on me with a pipe, I don't like to forget about it, let it drop." He stared at her some more. "You want to come along with me, you can. You can search for Bobby and I'll chase my man with the pipe." Thinking, *Let's hope they're not the same guy.*

He waited for her answer. "There's something," she said and stopped. "I need to tell you something."

"Fire away."

"The first time we talked, when we met in that bar and you asked me questions?"

"And you gave me no answers."

She looked at him straight. "I was there because Rex wanted me to find out what you were doing."

Jack said, "I figured that."

"You *knew*?"

"First you won't talk to me. Then you get a phone call and you go to the back of the Melon Patch Ranch, where, incidentally, Rex's office is. Then you *will* talk to me. I never said I was the sharpest guy in the world, but, hey . . . "

"When I found out Bobby might be involved I—"

"Switched sides."

Sally squared to face him, the bleached blue eyes beaming in. "Just out of curiosity," she said. "How do you know I'm not still checking you out for Rex?"

Jack shrugged. "Sometimes I have hunches."

"And you follow them?"

"Probably more than I should."

"What are they telling you now?"

She was a couple of feet from him. Jack gave a slight push with one foot and the chair rolled smoothly toward her. He stood, put his arms around her, and kissed her.

Sally clutched his shirt and pulled him closer. He felt her yanking at the fabric and heard his buttons pop. His shirt fell open. She peeled her sweater off over her head.

Jack lowered her onto the desk. As he straddled her, on his knees, he heard some clattering and banging, and then someone humming. He looked toward the door. A cleaning woman in a powder-blue smock was going over the outer office lamps with a feather duster. "Let's get out of here," he whispered.

They collected their coats without a word. He took her hand and they walked from the office. After they had stepped into the elevator and the doors had shut, just as the car started its descent, Sally reached past him and flipped the switch that said EMERGENCY STOP.

She moved away from him, almost to the opposite wall, and pulled her sweater off again. Her shoes came off with a kick of each foot. She unbuttoned her jeans, hooked her thumbs in the waistband, and dropped the jeans and her red panties together.

Sally stepped from the clothing bunched at her feet and came to him. Her nails raked across his shoulders and back as she pulled his shirt from him. She knelt to help him get his pants off, and stayed down.

After a couple of minutes or so, Jack couldn't be sure, a man's tinny voice came from the small speaker next to the elevator's control panel. "Building security," the voice said. "Everything all right in there?"

Sally stopped what she was doing long enough to say, "We're fine."

"My office doesn't have an elevator," Jack said. They were on the sidewalk in front of Greenie's 24-HR Coffee Shop.

"We'll work something out," Sally said. She looked up at the green neon frog. "Your office is in a restaurant?"

"Second floor." He pointed. "Suite Number Two in the Greenie's Building. Two-hundred-fifty square feet at one-seventy-five a month, plus utilities. Great view of the thrift shop across the street. At night you can kill the lights and watch the frog flash on and off."

Jack led her to the plate-glass door between the coffee shop and Melda's Hair & Nails. He unlocked the door and the two of them climbed the carpeted stairs together. "Two of the four offices up here are vacant," Jack said as they topped the stairway and turned into a narrow hallway. "The one next to me is occupied by Theo Fowler and Associates." He tapped the lettering on the door as they passed.

"Who's that?"

"No idea in the world. I've yet to see Theo Fowler. Or his associates. The closest I've come is one night when I heard somebody moving around in there. I knocked on the door, figuring I'd introduce myself, get to know my neighbor. But nobody would answer."

He stopped at the door that said J. FLIPPO in white stick-on letters and found the right key. "I asked Greenie about him once. He just shrugged and said it's some old guy who mails the rent in." Jack turned the key in the lock, swung the door open, and flipped on the light. "Make yourself at home," he said as he bent to pick up the mail that had been dropped through the slot.

Sally toured the walls, looking at Jack's law school diploma, his private investigator's license, a calendar from a Mexican restaurant, and some photographs he had taken. In one corner of the room leaned a bag of golf clubs. On his desktop was a lamp whose base was a bust of Elvis. The lightbulb screwed into the top of his head, making the King look like a cartoon character with an idea.

"Sometimes when I'm not doing anything else, I sit here and imagine the life story of Theo Fowler." Jack shuffled through the mail and tossed most of it in the trash. "I'm thinking maybe he's a World War Two vet, still haunted by what happened on some tiny island in the Pacific. Still sees the faces of the men he killed, that sort of thing. Has trouble with the bottle, lives off his pension. Keeps telling the wife he's going to sober up and get his consulting business going. Every morning he leaves the house, promising her he'll go to his office, but he hits the bars instead."

Sally stopped in front of a photo of a man with big

muscles, no shirt, and two Christmas tree ornaments hanging from his nipple rings. Jack said, "That's Lawrence Bird, aka Tweety, caught in a holiday mood . . . I usually take that one down when I know clients are coming in."

"Some picture."

"Tweety runs a motorcycle shop on South Lamar. Couple of years ago a cop makes a traffic stop in front of Tweety's place, there's a tussle between the cop and the perp, and the perp gets hold of the cop's gun. Tweety grabs him, grabs him so hard he breaks the perp's neck. So they have a big City Hall ceremony to honor Tweety for saving the cop's life. The mayor gives Tweety a plaque. Mayor says, Mr. Bird, tell us in your own words what you did. Tweety leans over the microphone and says, Mr. Mayor, I basically eighty-sixed the motherfucker."

Sally moved a stack of newspapers to the floor and sat on the couch. Floated down, it seemed to Jack. She said, "You just have a thing for stray dogs, don't you?"

Jack put the rest of the mail on the desk. "I won't tell Tweety you called him that."

"I wasn't talking about him."

"You know what I'm wondering?" he said, moving to the switch by the door. "I'm wondering what you would look like on that couch with no clothes on, with the green frog blinking on and off."

"Only one way to find out."

The earth didn't move as they made love, but the couch did. Its wooden armrest rattled the wall with each thrust. One framed photograph fell straight to the floor. Another dropped near Jack's head. He pushed it aside and heard glass break.

Sally was so loud that Jack was glad Theo Fowler wasn't in. He would have been on the phone to the police by now, reporting a beating next door. She quieted herself by biting Jack's shoulder.

When it was over he pulled himself from her and felt her shudder. Sticky skins were peeled apart, arms and legs were untangled. Jack climbed from the couch and went to his desk wondering if he would need stitches for his shoulder. He turned on the desk lamp and searched a drawer for some paper towels to apply to his wound.

A gray metal cabinet had a small mirror hanging on the inside door. Jack studied his back in it. Sally's nails had cut red lines, thin trails of blood, from his backbone out. He looked like someone who had been symmetrically whipped. He closed the cabinet and glanced about the room. Shards of glass lay on the floor, next to a pair of pants turned inside out. Sally seemed to have been thrown onto the couch, unconscious. One of her legs extended past the edge of a cushion. Her panties hung from her ankle. The face of the Elvis lamp was turned toward her. Jack began to sing "Love Me Tender."

After a while Sally managed to open her eyes and sit up. "You doing okay?" Jack said.

"You know, you make love like a stupid person. That's a compliment."

The ten o'clock news was on the TV when Jack walked into Greenie's and ordered two coffees to go. Sally had just about finished dressing by the time he made it back upstairs. Jack took her coffee from the bag and set it on the desk. "Listen, I was thinking on the way upstairs . . .

How well do you know Baby Echols?"

"We're not best friends, if that's what you're asking. She used to work at the Melon Patch, but that was before my time. I catch her every now and then when she comes down to see Rex about something. We've talked a few times, but nothing serious."

Jack pried the lid off his coffee, which smelled like yesterday's. "Mostly I know her through Bobby," Sally said. "He said a few things."

"Like?"

"Well . . . " Sally smoothed her sweater. "She used to tell Bobby she hated Rex and she didn't know why she'd ever married him, and the only reason she stayed with Rex was that he gave her money. Baby didn't like to work."

"Why work when you can swim all day and shoot bottles?"

"She wanted Bobby, though. He said he'd never been with anybody as crazy for him as Baby was. She'd divorce Rex in a second if Bobby would marry her."

"It must be love. Bobby doesn't have a swimming pool."

"No way he was going to marry Baby. He was just fooling around . . . He never told her that, though."

Jack was about to say something but wasn't sure what. His thoughts were like birds on a wire. One moved and they all flew away. He gave up on the coffee and tried to rub the sand from his eyes. "I'm sorry, I'm running on empty."

Sally rose from the chair and put her arm around him. "I'll get a cab home."

"I'll drive you . . . Before we go, though, try one thing. Call Baby and ask her if she's heard from Bobby. She might want to talk."

Sally began to page through the phone book on his desk. "Maybe we'll catch her at home."

He picked up broken glass while Sally found the number and dialed. "Hi, Baby, it's Sally Danvers. How are you? . . . Uh-huh . . . Oh, I know, winter is the worst for dryness . . . Have you been swimming a lot? Because that makes it even worse . . . Uh-huh . . . "

Jack stood, shards of glass in his hand, and listened to several minutes of chitchat about problem skin. He dumped the glass in the garbage can during a seminar on bath oils. He lay on the couch while they worked through a crisis involving pool chlorine and hair coloring.

Finally Sally said to the phone, "Listen, I need to ask you something." Jack sat up. Sally said, "Baby, I was wondering if you've seen Bobby Slater. I have something I—"

Sally was silent for a few seconds, the phone to her ear, then placed the handset gently into its cradle. "Well?" Jack said.

"That's a new one." Sally lifted her eyes to meet his. "Nobody's ever threatened to kill me before."

"Let's go out the back way," Jack said. "It'll be shorter." He led her down the first-floor hallway to a windowless door beneath a red EXIT sign. It opened onto the parking lot behind Greenie's.

"The place has filled up since we got here," Sally said.

"All the nighthawks have to roost somewhere." Jack

fished in his pocket for his keys. "Most nights I'm right in there with them."

They reached his truck and Jack unlocked the passenger door. As he started to open it Sally kissed him on the neck, then the chin, then the mouth. Jack broke it off when he felt a bright light shining on them.

A car's high beams, he thought as he pulled away from her. No, he figured as he turned to look, a heavy-duty flashlight. Only as he began to move toward it, blinking and shielding his eyes with his hand, did he see it belonged to a man with a video camera.

The camera was fifteen or twenty feet from him. Jack advanced. The man killed his light and ran. Jack recognized the shaved head, ripped jeans, and lace-up boots.

"You better run," Jack yelled as the man jumped into the open door of a waiting van. The van burned out of the parking lot and down the street, with a couple of toots on the horn as it went.

Jack watched it disappear into traffic, shook his head, and walked back to Sally. "I have a fair idea what that was all about, if you really want to know."

She took his hands in hers. "Let me ask you something," she said. "Are all your days like this?"

"Stay here tonight," Sally told him. They were climbing the steps to her apartment.

"You persuaded me," Jack said.

He watched her unlock the door, push it open, then heard her say, "Oh, hi, April."

Jack followed Sally in. April lay on the couch in panties and a T-shirt, watching TV. "Guess what he did this time," April said.

Sally put her purse on a table and took off her coat. "Who?"

"My roommate's boyfriend. The fabulous Tom. Guess what he did now."

"Tell me."

"I get home and he's in the kitchen. He's got nothin' on except these purple bikini briefs, but you'd think he's wearin' a sweater, the hair on his back."

Jack laid his jacket over a chair and leaned against the wall, trying to remember when he'd last had some decent sleep. April pulled a cigarette from her purse. Sally motioned for one of her own. "Did I tell you about his nostrils?" April said. She held her thumb and forefinger an inch apart. "This long, I swear. You could fit fifty-cent pieces in them."

Sally reached for a match. April leaned forward for a light from her. "I walk in and he says, 'Hey, babe, you're just in time.' I'm like, 'Just in time for what, fabulous Tom?' He gets this big grin, and he goes, 'Just in time for a Tom sandwich. You two girls can be the bread.'"

Sally shook her head and blew some smoke toward the ceiling. "Where's your roommate during all this?"

"Asleep, I guess. All I know is, fabulous Tom's in the kitchen talkin' about a sandwich. And I'm like, 'All night long I got guys puttin' their hands on me, and now I'm supposed to jump for a triple play with you? In your dreams, buddy.' Then he kinda wiggles his hips like this, and he goes, 'Babe, I got what you want.' These briefs he's wearin' show everything he's got, and it's not what I want, believe me. I mean, he's shakin' this little weenie at me, it's like an acorn. So just before I walk out the door, I tell him, 'Dude, let me know if that acorn ever grows into a tree.'"

April and Sally laughed together. "You shoulda seen his face after I laid that on him . . . Anyway, Sally, you mind if I hang here tonight?"

"Stay as long as you want." Sally stood and went to the kitchen for a glass of water, kissing Jack on the cheek as she passed.

April followed her and turned her purse upside down on the butcher-block table. "I'm gonna watch TV for a little, if that's okay, while I wait for my sleepin' pills to kick in." She poked through her pile on the table—lipstick, eyeliner, cotton balls, a Tampax, tissues, the night's tips, hair-pins, a candy cane, cigarettes, and a keychain with a tag that read, DRINK 'TIL HE'S CUTE. "If I even remembered to bring my pills. Here we go. I tell you, I have really had the trouble gettin' to sleep lately."

"What's this?" Sally said. Jack watched her pick up a shiny piece of paper, folded in half, that had come from April's purse. Sally looked at pictures of palm trees and read, "'It's better in the Bahamas.'" She returned it to the table. "That looks nice. You taking a trip?"

"Oh, that." April put a yellow tablet on her tongue, motioned for Sally's glass of water, and swallowed. "This guy I know wants to take me to some islands. I'm like, 'Sure, whatever.'"

"Sounds like fun," Sally said. She set the empty glass in the sink, went to Jack, and took his hand.

"He keeps sayin' any day now he's gonna come into a whole load of money. He's gonna get us a house on the beach where we can live."

"Send me a postcard," Sally said as she and Jack crossed the living room.

"Yeah, well, you know how these guys are, always tellin' you they're gonna do this and that." April went to the coffee table for the remote control. "You ever dated a guy who's a cop?"

Sally shook her head. "Uh-uh."

"Me neither," Jack said.

April skipped through the channels. "I don't know what it is about cops. Every one I've ever been with had some kind of wild scheme he was gonna work. Why do you think that is?"

Jack leaned against the corner at the hallway entrance. Fatigue was starting to weigh on him like a heavy coat. "Don't know," Sally said.

April paused at a hair care infomercial. "This one can't stop talkin' about the beach. The beach and the boat he's gonna buy. Man, does he go on and on about that. At least I guess that's what he's talkin' about. I just about have to turn up my hearin' aid to make it all out."

"I hope you have a nice time." Sally started down the hall.

"Good night," Jack said as he followed.

They undressed each other in Sally's bedroom and left their clothes in a pile on the floor. Jack sank into the bed first, and Sally crawled on top and gripped him with her thighs. When she came she dug her nails into his chest. "We keep seeing each other," Jack said when it was over, "I'll need a transfusion."

She laughed and rolled away. Jack lay in the dark, eyes closed, waiting for sleep to settle over him. He recalled the day's events in random pieces darting in and out—flashes of color, snatches of feeling, fragments of conversation.

"Wait a fucking minute." He sat up straight, blinking hard. "April has a hearing aid?"

28 "A red folder, that's all you know?" Jack asked.

"In Rex's office?" Sally said.

April with the remote cruised past a Mexican soap opera and an English soccer game before stopping at a documentary on circus freaks. "Oh, my God, look at that. No way. That's gotta be a fake ... What Loyce said was, it's in a red folder, and it's in Rex's office, and it's got all the poop about Bobby Slater and Baby." She glanced at Jack. "Hey, I can't believe you know Sheriff Loyce, too. Small world, huh?"

Sally tugged on Jack's arm, pulling him into the kitchen. The clock on the oven said it was after three in the morning. "Rex has a burglar alarm on the building," she told him.

"No surprise in that neighborhood." Jack rubbed his eyes. "That leaves us with broad daylight. We get some sleep and we handle it in the morning."

It took them about five minutes to decide who would do what.

*   *   *

"I frigging love this shot we got last night," Tony Angel said. He reached into a box beneath the van's front seats and held up a videocassette. Its label, written in pencil, said *Jack Flippo Surv. Project*. "The two of them making out in the parking lot. Unbelievable."

"Swapping spit," Mitch said. "Tongue wrestling."

"And then the jerkoff comes running after you, he's gonna bust your chops, what a segment." Tony sat in the driver's seat, watching the front of the house. Mitch slumped in a lawn chair at the back of the van, reading a Spider-Man comic. "You know what I'm thinking?" Tony said. He looked in the rearview mirror. "Yo, Mitch, wake up. I said, do you know what I'm thinking?"

"Oh, man, that's a tough one."

"I'm thinking that today, Mitch, instead of following the jerkoff? You with me here? Instead of the jerkoff, we follow the babe. Give her a bigger role in this project."

"We tail the piece of tail," Mitch said.

"That's what I'm thinking."

The midmorning sun shone through the driver's side window, warming Tony's thighs and making his black leather pants give off the smell of hide. Tony was still cheesed about his hair, but he wasn't feeling too bad, really. Could be worse, you thought about it.

Two years had passed since Caesar's told him to pack his bags. All that shit about phonied receipts, they couldn't prove a thing. But when those guys tell you to hit the road . . .

Tony ends up in Texas, and six months later he's facing charges. What kind of state calls it a frigging crime to make a secret video in your own condo of a slut who *vol-*

unteers to take off her clothes and hop in the sack? So what if he showed it to some friends at a party?

Actually, it worked out. No jail time, just three months of cleaning toilets at the funny farm. Which is where he runs into Mitch. They get to talking in the TV room. Turns out Mitch has a great-grandfather who's full-blooded Indian, almost.

Make that Native American. Tony helps Mitch fill out the application. Project: The Native American Video Artist in the Urban Wilderness. Next thing you know, just about the time the doctors give Mitch his release, twenty-five grand in U.S. government grant money comes in the mail. And Tony Angel Productions, with Mitch Cooper a newly installed corporate officer, is in business.

"That's what I'm thinking," Tony said again from the front seat of the van. "Today we follow the babe."

"On the job," Mitch said from the back, head buried in Spider-Man. Tony watched the house and tried to see how still he could sit. He imagined himself a wild animal, a predator, waiting until the exact right moment to pounce on his prey. The minutes floated by, with the only sound the repeated rasp and click of Mitch's disposable lighter. With Tony thinking it was all kind of relaxing if you did it right.

"Shit!" Mitch shouted.

Tony jerked around to see Mitch leaping from the chair and knocking flames from his lap. The burning comic book fell to the floor, and Mitch stamped out the fire with his boots.

"Man," Mitch said and shook his head. "Now I'm not gonna know how it ends."

*   *   *

Jack walked into the Melon Patch Ranch around twelve-fifteen, cruising past a handful of customers drinking lunch. Sally was behind the bar. He caught her eye just before he went through the Employees Only door at the back of the room.

In the harsh light of the hallway he walked past the time clock and the Department of Labor posters. He found Rex at his desk, checking invoices. Rex raised his dark glasses in Jack's direction and said, "The hell you want?"

Jack stood in the doorway. "I thought we'd talk."

"About what?"

"I went out to Baggett County the other night, and while I was there somebody tried to send me a message. Wrapped in a pipe."

Rex grinned. "Sounds like you tangled with some bad boys."

Jack glanced up and down the hallway, then turned back to Rex. "It made me see things in a different light."

Rex tossed his pen onto his desk, folded his arms, and leaned back. "Uh-huh," he said.

"I work hard for my clients, and they usually pay me pretty well. No medical coverage, though. If I happened to get my legs or ribs or arms broken, I'd have to foot that bill myself."

"That could cost you, the way them damn doctors run it up."

Jack took a step into the room. "Like I said, the whole experience made me look at this case of yours in a new light. I started thinking, maybe I'm not being fair here. You know, I was just about to file my report to Continental Centurion, and I wondered if I wasn't being a little too harsh in my assessments. You know what I mean?"

Rex chewed some air and said, "Not yet."

Jack dropped his voice. "Last time I was in here you mentioned a possible arrangement. Between you and me."

They stared at each other. Jack could hear the bass notes from the big speakers shaking the walls. Rex took a big breath and let it out. He put his hands on the desk and drummed. "All right," he said, "I can go five thou—"

"Wait, wait," Jack said, holding up a hand. "Hang on. Before you go any further, let me tell you something. There's two things I am deathly afraid of. One of them is snakes—"

"What in the *fuck* are you talkin' about?"

"—and the other is tape recorders. Know what I'm saying?"

Rex waved a backhand at the room. "They ain't no tape recorders in here, for cryin' out loud."

"You might as well point to the woods and tell me there's no snakes in there. Both of them hide pretty well."

Rex sighed and shook his head. "You are one strange booger, you know that?"

Jack stepped to the desk, put his palms flat on it, and leaned close to Rex. "I'm ready to talk," he said. "I'm ready to do it right now. Just not in here."

Darnell the bouncer was on parking lot patrol. He did it every day, two or three times. Went out and strolled the pavement, making sure everything was on the up and up. He didn't mind it, especially on a sunny day like this one. It gave him a chance to take some fresh air, kept his bad knee from getting too stiff.

He gazed across Northwest Highway and watched a jet fly low over Bachman Lake on its way to Love Field. Darnell stretched, cracked his knuckles, and thought about the lady he'd been with the night before. Energetic little thing. He stretched again and turned toward the Melon Patch. That was when he saw the van, parked sideways across a couple of spaces with its sliding door open.

Darnell wandered over, hearing voices as he came closer. He peered in through the side doorway and saw two men standing at the rear of the van, their backs to him, fiddling with a video camera. The back door of the van was cracked open, with the camera pointed at the Melon Patch.

One of the men had strange-looking hair, a baggy sweater, black leather pants, and rings. Darnell heard him say, "The frigging Melon Patch Ranch, can you believe it? Let's get the sign, then pull back for the whole building."

The other man, a younger one, wore lots of ripped denim and had a shaved head. That no-hair bit looked pretty good on brothers, Darnell thought, but on white boys it put him in mind of an egg that needed cracking.

"Gentlemen," Darnell said. They both jumped. Darnell had to laugh as he stepped into the van. "About to take some pictures?" He looked at the bald one. "What's up, Li'l Egghead?"

"The fuck you want?" said the one in the leather pants. Darnell thought, That's the one'll be trouble.

"Want to know what is with the camera." Darnell held out a hand. "Let's have us a look."

"Get lost," said Leather Pants.

"What's the deal here, man?" Darnell said, keeping his

hand out, wiggling his fingers. "You dudes from some other bar that gots the girls with big jugs? Checkin' out the competition?"

"You hear what I said, Darkman? Take a hike."

"No problem." Darnell smiled. "Be happy to soon as I get a look at that camera."

The two dudes weren't moving to help him, so Darnell went for the tripod. "Hey," Leather Pants said as he reached across and tried to knock Darnell's hand away.

Darnell grabbed his wrist. "Bad move, man." He twisted the arm, turning the man around, the arm straight out behind him now. Darnell brought his left hand down in a chopping motion, his fist connecting at the back of the elbow. He heard a snap, then a scream. Darnell let go of the wrist and the dude dropped to the floor.

Li'l Egghead just watched. Bald head, big eyes. "Now his arm swing both ways," Darnell said, unscrewing the camera from the tripod. "Just like a gate."

Darnell moved back toward the side door as he pulled the tape cassette from the camera. "Believe I'll take this tape," he said. "But you can have the camera back." He tossed it out the doorway, onto the parking lot. "Oops."

A box between the front seats contained another cassette. Darnell took that tape, too. "Y'all have a nice day, now," he said as he stepped from the van.

"That way." Rex pointed down the hallway. "Out that door." Jack went first, pushing on the chrome-plated bar across the door and stepping into sunshine. They were in the alley behind the Melon Patch. "This good enough for you?" Rex said. "You wanna search the garbage cans, make sure there's no hidden cameras?"

Jack looked around. "This is exactly what I had in mind."

"Oh, I am *so* glad you're happy. Are you ready to deal now? Or do you need to check for spy satellites?"

Jack cleared his throat. "As I was saying in your office, my visit to Baggett the other night—well, it transformed my thinking on this whole affair. I guess what I'm trying to say is it made me examine what I'm doing here. Let me tell you a little bit about myself and I think you'll understand—"

"Is this a fuckin' speech?" Rex spread his arms. "I thought we come out here to do a deal."

"This is not easy for me, all right?" Jack stepped closer to him. "It's not the normal way I do business. Understand? But there's a different set of circumstances this time, you know what I'm saying?"

"Hell, no."

"And because it's different, it's important to me to throw everything on the table, let you see where I'm coming from, and then we can negotiate our deal."

Rex looked at his watch. "I'll give you one damn minute."

"I need more than that."

"Man, you're a weird one." Rex let out a breath, shook his head, and adjusted his hat. "Awright," he said, "talk fast."

Sally had peered down the hallway and seen Rex's back as he went out the door to the alley. Now she was in his office, going through his desk. There were plenty of folders, but no red ones. She found inventory sheets, sales figures, payroll records, and song lyrics, but nothing that talked about Baby and Bobby. She was squatting as she pulled open the last desk drawer. Inside were several rolls of pennies and a gun.

She closed the drawer, stood, and steadied herself. Jack had said he could probably give her five minutes, but she had forgotten to check her watch when she started. She moved to a file cabinet behind the desk, her back to the door. The top drawer was crammed with papers and envelopes, and she riffled through it. Nothing of interest there, so she moved to the middle one.

"What's up, Miss Sally?" She whirled to see Darnell filling up the doorway. "Where the man at?"

"Rex? He should be back any minute now. Can I help you?"

Darnell showed her two videotape cassettes. "Droppin' these off for him."

"Well . . . " Sally swallowed. "If you want to just leave them on the desk, I'll make sure he gets them."

Darnell looked at the tapes in his hands, then back at Sally. "What you doin' in here, anyway?"

"Rex had a lot of paperwork he needed some help with. So"—she smiled—"I sorta volunteered."

"Uh-huh." Darnell glanced over his shoulder. "I just come past the bar and two of the girls was complainin' they couldn't get they drink orders." Darnell smiled. "Just thought you'd like to know."

"Oh, thanks." Sally shut the middle drawer. "Would you do me a favor, Darnell? Go tell them I'm almost finished, and I'll be right out?"

Darnell squinted. "Where you say Rex at?"

"I think he just went to the bathroom or something.

Darnell, please? Tell the girls I'll be right there to get their drinks? Please?"

He waited, then nodded. "Okay." He held the tapes up. "I'll drop these back for Rex later."

Darnell turned and left. Sally listened for his footsteps down the hall, trying to hear them over her own breathing. She went to the doorway and peeked around it to make sure he was gone.

Back at the cabinet, she opened the last drawer. The red file was the first thing she saw.

29 "I'm tired of hearin' your life story," Rex said. "Like I said I don't know how long ago, five thousand dollars. That's my offer."

Jack drew air through his teeth and blew it out. He said, "Hmm," waited, then "Hmm" again.

"Lemme ask you one question," Rex said. "You got a worm in your brain?"

"Now let's get this straight." Jack checked his watch. They had been in the alley for seven minutes. He had meant to put himself between Rex and the door, but Rex had not moved far enough into the alley. "Let me get this straight, now. Just so we understand each other. You want me to file a report to the Continental Centurion insurance company that states, in regard to the policy held by one Rex Echols of Dallas, Texas, concerning key man coverage and the drowning death of one Mingo Gideon in Baggett County, Texas—"

"This is un-fuckin'-believable."

"—that I, the investigator retained by the company,

believe the claim to be legitimate. That all official paper-work is in order and the drowning, in my experienced judgment, was accidental."

"How about that, folks?" Rex gestured and glanced from side to side as if he had an audience. "Let's give him a big hand, 'cause the man finally said something." He clapped three times.

"Now in return, you"—Jack pointed—"promise to do . . . what?"

Rex raised one hand, fingers spread. "Can you count that high? I keep sayin' it, but you don't seem to hear. So count each finger I'm holdin' up, includin' the thumb, then put a thousand on the end of it. Soon as I get paid, that's what I give to you."

"Now, let me get this straight," Jack said.

"Sheeyit." Rex went for the door. "Get it straight by yourself."

Jack reached for him and grabbed the sleeve of his shirt. "One more thing," Jack said.

Rex slapped Jack's hand away and kept moving. "No more things," he said as he pulled the door open. "You wanna talk about anything else, it'll be inside."

Jack trailed Rex down the hallway, right behind him as he made the turn into his office, ready to come down on the back of Rex's head if Sally were still there.

Rex dropped into his chair with a hiss from the cushion. "When you gonna file this report to the inshurnce company?"

Jack stood before the desk. "Could be tomorrow, I don't know."

"How about today? Today's a good day. The quicker I

see my money, the quicker you get yours. Even you oughtta be able to figure that."

"There is one other thing we need to talk about."

"Oh, boy." He shook his head. "Here we go again, and we ain't even in the alley. I thought you was afraid of tape recorders in here."

"I got over it," Jack said.

"Then what the hell we had to spend all that time outside for?"

"Listen, there's still the matter of this missing witness, Bobby Slater. I never did get to talk to him."

"I told you, he quit. He left and never come back. Gone with the wind. How's that any big deal, anyway?"

"Well, it's a potential problem. Say I put in my report that one of the chief eyewitnesses can't be found. That might make the company suspicious."

"You need to talk to Bobby Slater?" Rex stood and patted his chest. "Fine. I'm Bobby Slater, and this here's what I have to say. Everything that Rex Echols tells you is A-okay by me." Rex sat down again. "There. Happy?"

Jack rubbed his chin. "That might do it. Problem is, what if somewhere down the road the real Bobby Slater surfaces and starts telling a different story?"

Rex grinned. "That won't happen."

"How do you know?"

"Trust me," Rex said.

They met outside her apartment. "I hid it under the back of my shirt and waltzed straight out of the Melon Patch," Sally said. "Straight out, like it was no big deal. When I was sure nobody was looking I locked it in my trunk, and I went back inside. I started working the bar again as if nothing was any different." She was smiling and talking fast as they climbed the stairs. "It was so easy I couldn't believe it."

Jack took the folder from her. "Then what? You didn't just walk off the job, did you?"

Sally unlocked the door. "No, I did what we said. I waited until you were gone and then I went to Rex and told him I was sick."

"You told him that."

"I said I had cramps. He just winced and waved me away."

They walked into the apartment. Jack set the folder on the table in the kitchen and shook his head. "We didn't work this through well enough. You should have waited a few hours before checking out. If Rex thinks hard enough about it he'll put us together."

"Let's see what's in there," she said, pulling a chair close to the table. "All the way home I wanted to stop and read it."

Jack took the other chair. "How long were you in Rex's office?"

"I don't know. Come on, let's get started."

"You didn't keep track?"

"Hey, I was too busy to look at my watch."

"You were supposed to be out in five minutes, file or no file. That was the deal."

"I got what we were after, so what's the problem?"

She started to open the folder but Jack put his hand on it. "Did anybody see you?" he said.

She waited a couple of seconds. "No."

"You're not sure."

"Yes, I am."

"Who saw you?"

"Nobody saw me. I told you the first time, all right?"

"Look, sooner or later Rex is going to figure out this file is missing." Jack tapped the folder with his finger. "When that happens he'll go off like a rocket. If he knows you're the one who did it—"

"He'll come after me."

"That's right. Even if he still thinks he's bought me off, he'll come roaring after you."

"Well, nobody saw me."

"If there's any chance, *any*, then we need to get you out of town right now. You can go visit Texas City or something, anywhere. But you need to be gone."

She leaned toward him, her face only a few inches from his. "For the last time, nobody saw me." They stared at each other until Sally broke away and slipped the folder from under Jack's hand.

Jack watched her open it, saw her eyes move back and forth as they followed her finger down the page. "This is incredible," she said. "Look at this stuff. You know, I've had a feeling, ever since April told us about this. I knew this would get us rolling, if we could only get our hands on it. And now we have it. This is great. You can't beat this."

She glanced up from the page with a giddy face that fell some when she saw Jack. "What's your problem?" she said.

"I've got a feeling, too, and mine's telling me we've made some kind of mistake here. Or we're about to."

Sally grimaced and cocked her head, looking irritated,

asking a question in a tone that said she didn't want an answer. "Like what, exactly?"

"That's what I'm trying to figure out," Jack said.

"Well, you keep figuring," Sally stood and moved toward the phone. "I'm calling Baby Echols. If this stuff won't make her talk to us, nothing will."

At three in the afternoon, Tony and Mitch walked out of the Parkland emergency room. Tony had his left arm in a cast, a bottle of prescription pain pills, and a referral to an orthopedic surgeon. "That frigging gorilla was on a mission," Tony said.

Mitch flicked his lighter on and off as they crossed the parking lot. "Man, that guy was big," he said when they were in the van.

"He was a fucking guided missile sent by someone. Search your imagination and take a wild guess who."

"You see the size of his arms?"

"Hey, Mitch, I was the *victim* of those arms. You forget that already?"

"Arms bigger than Mister T's, I bet." Mitch dropped his voice. "*I pity the fool.*"

"You know what happened, Mitch? I'll tell you what happened. Tony Angel was getting too close. The jerkoff heard Tony Angel's footsteps."

"You hungry, man?" Mitch turned onto Mockingbird. "I think there's a McDonald's down here."

Tony closed his eyes. "You can't believe how fucking much this hurts. It even hurts to breathe. I need more medicine." He clutched the pills in his right hand. "Get me something to drink."

"There it is," Mitch said. "The golden arches."

Tony stayed silent while they waited in the drive-thru line. He half dozed as Mitch ordered a Coke and a Happy Meal. He screamed when Mitch—saying, "Here you go, man"—nudged his left arm with the Coke.

Mitch put a hand over his ear with the cross hanging from it. "Man, you scream like a girl."

"Don't touch me. Ever again, you hear me? You touch me again and I take my one good hand and wrap it around your throat."

"Here's a good place." Mitch backed the van into a spot on the McDonald's lot. He turned off the engine and inspected his Happy Meal toy. "Oh, man, this sucks. Daffy Duck in a car again. They're supposed to change these."

"That's the second time he's come after me." Tony took two pills. "All right, so he sent somebody else this time, he's still behind it. Don't doubt it for a second. He's a frigging maniac, that guy."

"I'm gonna complain, man." Mitch held the Daffy Duck figure in front of him. "Supposed to be a new one like every week."

"Well, he's about to find out Tony Angel won't roll over. You understand? I'm not just gonna pay the guy back, I'm gonna get good video out of it, too. Mitch, you listening to me?"

The smell of burning plastic filled the van. Tony turned to see Mitch melting the front end of Daffy Duck's car. They both stared at the flame.

30 "Maybe Baby went to her other house," Sally said. "I've been trying her at home in Dallas for, what, two or three hours now? Maybe she went out to Baggett." She raised herself from the bed, picked up the phone, and turned to Jack before dialing. "What's the area code out there?"

Jack couldn't remember. He watched Sally leave the bed and walk out of the room, then come back half a minute later with the phone book. She stood a few feet from the bed, naked, turning pages. "It should tell in here, shouldn't it? Isn't there some kind of map?"

"They don't make it easy for you."

"Where is Baggett, anyway?"

"Nowhere, that's where. Give me a minute, I'll help you look when I get back." Jack rolled out of bed, stepped over their clothes, and went down the hall to the bathroom. He used the toilet and washed his face. The warm water felt so good that he decided to take a quick shower. Then it was back to the bedroom. He couldn't have been gone more than ten minutes.

Sally was in bed waiting for him, lying on her elbows, her knees bent. "It's all set," she said.

"What's all set?"

"I talked to Baby. We're seeing her tonight."

He crawled into the bed next to her. "Slow down."

"I reached her at the house in Baggett. I just told her, Listen, Rex knows all about you and Bobby, and I can prove it, I've got all the reports right here, and I want to show them to you. Easy as that." She kissed Jack between his chest and his navel. "Soon as we show her those, she'll see that Bobby's in trouble. I think she'll help us then."

Jack lay on his back and looked at the ceiling. "Tell me we're not going to Baggett to see her."

"That's where she is."

"Call her back. Tell her to come here. She doesn't want to do that, tell her to meet us halfway. We'll rendezvous someplace fancy, like the Sulphur Springs Waffle House."

"Jack." Sally laid her hand where she had just kissed him. "Baby's scared to death. She's sure not coming to Dallas where Rex or his friends might see her."

"So we're going to Baggett where the sheriff can watch our every move? Put us in one of his reports to Rex?"

Sally smiled. "That's why we're not supposed to meet her until midnight. Nobody'll be watching then."

"Says who?"

"But just in case, she'll park her car in the back of her house."

Jack sat up. "We're going to a town that didn't leave me with a lot of pleasant memories last time I was there. The woman we're supposed to see—someone who carries a gun, don't forget—has threatened both of us."

She reached down, stroked his thigh, and took him in

her hand, as if she were holding him by his leash. "Think about it, Jack. What's the worst thing that could happen?"

"Baby could shoot somebody."

"No, I'm serious."

"So am I."

Rex was back at his desk, uncertain whether to feel good or not. Maybe the fix was in, and maybe it wasn't. He wouldn't know until he saw the actual report to the insurance company, and even then he couldn't be sure. The squirrel Flippo could show Rex one version and send the company another. Like the song said, The heart don't lie but the mouth's a different story.

"Got something for you."

Rex looked up to see Darnell in the doorway. "My man," Rex said.

Darnell stepped forward and set two videocassettes on Rex's desk. "Two motherfuckers out in the parking lot this afternoon playing with they camera. Had it pointed at the building and all."

"Who was it?"

"Don't know. Last I saw, one of 'em need a doctor."

Rex grinned. "You handled it, then."

"Took care a business."

"When was this? This afternoon?"

Darnell turned to leave but stopped halfway. "Don't know exactly the hour. About the time Miss Sally in here working."

Rex sat up. "In where working?"

Darnell waved a big hand. "In the office here. Doing stuff with all your papers and shit."

"Doing what with the papers?"

"Hey, how I'm supposed to know? It don't say Darnell on the door, last time I look."

"Where was I?" Rex said.

"The same thing I ask Miss Sally ... Hey, Rex, can't you keep track a your own self?" Darnell laughed and walked out. Talking to himself and laughing as he went down the hall. Saying, "Hey, Rex. Where Rex at? Heh-heh-heh. Rex done lost hisself ... "

Rex tried to think of a reason why Sally would be nosing through his office, and came up empty. He began to go through each drawer, looking for something missing or out of place. It took him about two minutes to discover that the red folder with Loyce Slapp's surveillance reports was gone.

He felt himself begin to tighten inside. Someone had mistaken him for a rube at the midway. Someone was trying to fire a torpedo into his dreamboat.

Rex reached into the bottom drawer of his desk and got his gun. Thinking, First stop is Miss Sally's house, to find out what the game is.

As he stood his eye caught the label on one of the videotapes. *Jack Flippo Surv. Project*, in pencil. "The fuck is this," he said out loud. Rex took it, crossed the room, and slid in into his VCR.

Most of the tape meant nothing to him. Nighttime shadows flickering against walls, a couple of minutes of feet moving along a sidewalk, and the view of traffic through a windshield.

Then he came to a shot taken at night: Two people, a man and a woman, standing beside the door of a pickup truck, kissing. Next, both of them looking up and blinking into the light. Rex didn't have to try hard to see who it was.

He swung his chair toward his desk. All his questions had been answered. The number he wanted was on a small sheet of paper in his wallet. He found it and picked up the phone.

"It's Rex," he said when there was an answer. "Somethin's come up. Get your ass to Dallas tonight."

Jack told Sally he would be back in a few hours to pick her up. He still wasn't happy about making the trip to Baggett, but admitted he had no better ideas. Truth was, if Baby Echols couldn't lead them to Bobby, the chances of finding him looked bleak. What do we do then? Sally had asked. We can watch for any credit card activity, Jack said, and keep checking with his family, or we can try to get the feds or the Texas Rangers interested in the case.

Beyond that, he said, you just about have to wait until Bobby decides to walk up and say hello. If he can, Sally said.

The red folder lay on the seat beside him as Jack drove toward his office. Half a dozen or so pages of typed, single-spaced cop porn: *Officer observed subjects engage in mutual oral sodomy on diving board for approximately ten minutes. Officer then observed subjects engage in genital copulation in same location, with male subject entering female subject from rear position. Copulation continued for approximately eight minutes.* Loyce Slapp liked to watch, and he liked to watch his watch, too.

Jack pulled into the back parking lot of Greenie's 24-HR. It was six-thirty, already dark, with the wind kicking up some. Greenie wasn't doing much dinner trade tonight. The lot was nearly empty.

He picked up the red file to take with him but left his coat in the truck. Upstairs, he went through his mail and checked his messages. He made a copy of the Loyce Slapp reports and tidied up. At just after seven he went down to the coffee shop to see if tonight's special was something he could handle.

Jack carried the red file and its original contents with him. Thinking it wouldn't hurt to have Greenie stash the file for him in the restaurant safe. Something might happen, you never knew.

31 "There it is." Tony pointed across the parking lot with his bottle of wine cooler, sloshing some on the van's seat. "Ready to die for Tony Angel Productions. Ready to— Mitch, where the fuck are you going?"

"I wanna drive around the block, make sure there's no police hanging." Mitch took a right and steered the van past Greenie's. "Don't you think we oughta check?"

"That's the thing about fire." Tony's words came out as if he had a swollen tongue. "I mean, Mitch, I can't believe I have to tell this to you, of all people, it fucking blows me away. Listen, are you listening to me? Fire don't wait around. Fire takes care of business right away, you hear what I'm saying? We start it, we get our tape, and we get outta here. The cops you're worried about? You know where they are, these frigging cops? They're off eating doughnuts."

Mitch flicked his lighter as he drove. "Man, those pills are making you talk funny."

"Give me some more. Stop driving and open this." He thrust the bottle of pills toward Mitch. "Are you frigging deaf? Help me out here."

"I can't stop in the middle of the street. I'll have a wreck."

"So, what, you're so worried about a frigging wreck you're gonna let me die? I gotta scream in pain over here before you do something? Screw it, I'll do it myself." Tony opened the bottle with his teeth, spit out the cap, tapped two pills into his mouth, and downed them by draining his wine cooler.

Mitch drove back to the parking lot behind Greenie's. "How're you gonna hold the camera?" he said.

"With my frigging hand. Give it to me and I'll show you. Where is it?"

Mitch stopped the van. "How should I know?"

"Give it to me." Tony snapped his fingers twice, then looked at them as if they had made a sound he never heard before.

"Tony, don't you remember? I took care of the gasoline and the rags. Then we stop by your house, I go in to take a dump, I come out, and I ask you did you get the other camera? I mean, we can't use the one we had, right? I mean, the Mister T guy took care of that. And then you tell me the other camera's in the van. In the van, that was your words."

Tony licked his lips. "I'm gonna frigging die from thirst. Get me another cooler."

Mitch put the van in park and stepped to the back. He pulled a bottle from a brown paper bag, opened it, and took it to Tony. More searching in bags produced a camera. "Okay, it's here," Mitch said.

Tony raised the wine cooler in a toast. "Next time maybe you'll listen."

"I listen," Mitch said. "But, man, you've been drinking those wine things all afternoon and taking those pills like candy. You know?"

Tony swallowed and smacked twice. "It makes me better. You don't believe me, I'll prove it. Give me the camera." Mitch handed it to him. "Now," Tony said, "give me the fire."

"That's gonna take a couple of minutes."

"Give me the fire in a couple of minutes, then." Tony sank back into his seat.

The van was parked parallel to the truck, about fifty feet away. The lot had a few other cars in it but no people. A couple of mercury vapor lamps on the back of Greenie's Office Building kept it from complete darkness.

Mitch looked around, then walked quickly to the truck and pried open the driver's-side vent window with a screwdriver. The glass shattered into pellets. When Mitch climbed back into the van Tony snapped his head forward and said, "How long I been asleep?"

Strips of bedsheet, tied together like a prisoner's escape rope, lay in the back, next to two cans of gasoline. Mitch took the cans to the pavement, removed the lid of one, and began stuffing the bedsheet in. Tony stirred, stood, and lurched toward the open door, stopping just short of a plunge to the ground. He looked toward Greenie's Office Building and announced, "I gotta piss."

Mitch pulled the gas-soaked strip of sheet out of the can and walked with one end to the truck. He began to stuff it through the broken vent. Tony opened the van's back doors and sang "Do You Think I'm Sexy?" as he peed. Steam billowed from the pool of urine on the pavement.

Moving fast, Mitch pushed the nozzle of the second can through the vent and poured a gallon of gasoline into the truck's cab. The smell of gas surrounded them. The rope of sheets ran down from the truck and straight along the pavement back to the van. Mitch said, "Ready for blastoff."

"Here's where we teach him not to fuck with Tony Angel. Here's where the jerkoff learns his lesson. Give me the camera, Mitch. And a cooler."

Mitch dropped his hands to his sides. "*You* had the camera. I gave it to you."

"And I put it down. So now it's your job, since you're the frigging production assistant, Mitch, to find it and bring it to me. Along with a cooler."

It took Mitch about twenty seconds to locate the camera and get the wine. He was starting to panic, saying, "The gas is evaporating. We can't wait."

Tony placed the camera at his feet, swallowed some wine, and said, "Let's see the lighter."

Mitch made huffing noises like a child about to cry. "But I was gonna light the fire. Come on, Tony, that's not fair. I mean, that's why I worked so hard, Tony. You gotta let me light the fire."

Tony propped himself against the edge of the van's doorway. "You think I'd steal the frigging pyro from the frigging maniac, Mitch?" He tossed the bottle out the door and bent for the camera. "Get a grip, all right? All I want is a shot of it before you have your fun."

It took a few seconds, but Mitch finally understood.

He jumped to the ground, pulled his lighter from his pocket, and held it aloft like a tiny torch. "Perfect," Tony said. "And now, ladies and gents, Mitch Cooper and His Dancing Flames."

Mitch knelt and touched the lighter's tip to the end of his homemade fuse. The flames leapt with a *whoosh* along the length of the sheets and into the truck. The cab exploded. Windows blew out, and the shock wave hit them. Mitch leaned, open-mouthed, against the van. "Oh," he moaned. "Oh."

Tony stood inside the van, camera rolling, shooting through the side doorway. "Start the engine," he yelled.

Mitch kept his eyes on the billowing, roaring orange flames, but felt his way to the door handle. He climbed in the front and rolled the window down, letting the heat wash over him.

"Pull away slow," Tony said. He kept shooting. The truck's back window popped, with nuggets of glass raining onto its metal bed.

Mitch groped for the ignition, his gaze still on the flames. "God," was all he could say.

"Pull away slow," Tony shouted. "The fuck are you doing?"

Tony kept shouting, and Mitch managed to shift the van into drive. But he did not move it until the red and blue lights of a police car began to sweep across the parking lot. Mitch broke out of his trance and hit the gas pedal hard. The acceleration mashed him against the seat.

Tony was still standing in the middle of the van, camera pointed toward the fire. The sudden motion jerked him toward the rear. He staggered, trying to keep his feet.

The back doors, left unlatched after he took his piss, blew open like loose shutters in a storm. Tony flew past them, out of the van, into the air. The van had driven out from under him. He was screaming when he hit the pavement.

He opened his eyes to see a policeman standing above him, badge shining orange as the truck burned. Tony lay on his side, half his face in a puddle. He thought it was blood until he smelled the urine.

"I got a broken arm," Tony moaned.

The policeman looked at the cast. "I can see that."

"I'm talking about the other one."

32 Jack was eating chicken and dumplings at Greenie's, black-eyed peas on the side, when he heard the fire engine's siren. Someone came in a minute or so later and said a car was in flames on the back parking lot. Jack ordered a piece of pecan pie. Someone else walked in and said it was a pickup truck burning. Jack ran outside.

The firefighters were still hosing the carcass down when he arrived. He didn't have to come close to see that it was a total loss, except for what he could get for the engine, four used tires, and some scrap metal.

Once Jack waded through the small crowd and identified himself as the owner, a cop with an open notebook walked over. He was a sergeant, in his fifties, bald and overweight, eyes incapable of surprise. Jack tried to remember if he'd ever seen him in court. The sergeant asked Jack's name, address, and the make and model of the truck. He wrote it all down, then flipped to a previous page. "You know an individual calling himself"—the sergeant checked his notes—"Tony Angel? Real name Anthony D'Angelo?"

Jack felt anger flash through him. "That piece of shit did this? Where is he?"

"We got him, him and his friend."

They watched the steam rising off the blackened truck. "You have insurance?" the sergeant said.

"Yeah. Five hundred deductible."

"Could be worse, then."

"It could always be worse," Jack said.

The sergeant wanted Jack's theory on why Anthony D'Angelo would do such a thing. A fire department investigator came up and asked him the same sort of questions. Jack gave them the only story he had: It all started with a former wife and an ex-ponytail. Then he thanked the crew of firefighters for what they had tried to do and went back into Greenie's to settle his check.

While he was waiting for his waitress he called Sally on a pay phone. We'll have to take your car to Baggett tonight, he told her. Got a little problem here, he said, with my truck overheating.

Jack left the front door to Greenie's Office Building unlocked for Sally and climbed the stairs. After rooting around in the files for his truck policy, he called his insurance agency and left a message on the answering machine, telling them where they could view the remains.

He switched on the Elvis desk lamp and reread his copy of the Loyce Slapp papers. For a while he rested his head on the back of the chair and closed his eyes.

The sound of footsteps coming down the hall pulled

him from his doze. It seemed too early for Sally, but maybe he had lost track of the time.

Jack switched off the lamp and stood. He looked to the doorway, smiling even before he saw her, ready to say, You won't believe what happened to my damn truck, you just won't believe it.

The person who came through the door was carrying a gun. It wasn't Sally. "Hey there, squirrel," Rex Echols said.

"Lots of excitement out there tonight," Rex said as he walked in. He had his hat on and his sunglasses off. His handgun was pointed at the middle of Jack's chest. "Big old fire and everything."

Jack stared at the gun, a semiautomatic the dull, dark color of a water moccasin. "What do you want here?"

"Goddamn, you don't stop with the questions, do you?" Rex's eyes darted around the office, then settled on Jack. "Come on around from the backside of that desk. No tellin' what you got back there." Rex motioned with the gun toward the couch. "Have yourself a seat over there. Come on, get after it. Don't make me get mean."

Jack went to the couch. Rex took the chair behind the desk. "Well, now," Rex said, "ain't this nice."

There was the sound of a cough from the hallway, a man's deep hack. Rex looked toward the doorway and spoke to someone Jack couldn't see, saying, "Check all the offices, make sure no one's here." Then to Jack, "That was some fire, wudn't it? Wanna know somethin' funny? We set out there in our car and watched them two dumbasses, whoever the hell they were, do the whole shebang. Start to finish. I said, Goddamn, they're gonna blow that truck up, and sure enough they did. I mean, we come lookin' for you, squirrel, and get a free show in the bargain. The hell was that all about, anyway?"

Jack didn't answer. "You get it burnt up for the inshurnce?" Rex said. "Probly woulda been a lot easier just to have it stole. I mean, them two boys didn't have a clue. You hire them? 'Cause if you did, get your money back, my advice."

A man came in. He stood just inside the doorway, coughing. "What I want to know," Rex said to the man, "is how you catch a cold when you spent the last three weeks locked up by yourself. Explain that one to me."

The man said nothing. He wore a blue nylon jacket, faded jeans, black leather gloves, and a blue ski mask with a little red ball on top. Who put on a ski mask, Jack thought, when it was forty degrees out? "You musta picked up them cold germs that one night you got outta the house," Rex said. He looked at Jack. "Hey, squirrel, you give my boy here a cold? Shame on you."

Jack said, "What are you talking about?" He got his answer when the man reached up and pulled off the ski mask, showing short dark hair, mournful brown eyes, and a long, narrow face with just enough lines to place him in his early thirties. Balls of blue lint from the ski mask clung to his three-or-four-day beard. A bandage lay diagonally over the bridge of his nose. Above his left brow was a purple bruise and a scab shaped like a check mark.

221

"You're the one," Jack said. He remembered the dark blur of the man's face when he had broken the chair across it at the Heart-o-the-Pines Lodge.

Rex laughed. "He's the one, all right. He's the fuckin' one and he's back for a second chance at you, squirrel. He mighta missed you once, but I believe this time he's got you pinned down."

The man coughed a couple of times and shut the door. Jack looked at Rex and said, "I thought we got all this worked out this afternoon. I thought we had a deal. What are you here for? We had it all worked out."

Rex took off his hat and fanned his face, the black gun still in his other hand. "You just don't stop tryin', do you, squirrel? I mean, you don't think I know by now that you and Miss Sally had a thing goin'?"

"Look, it doesn't matter now," Jack said, talking fast, bailing. "All that doesn't mean anything. Continental Centurion has already decided to pay you. You'll get your money."

Rex put his hat back on and looked at the other man. "This boy just says anything that pops into his head." Then, back to Jack, "I can't wait to hear what you're gonna tell me next."

"They sent a letter. It's a done deal, they're gonna pay you. It doesn't matter what I tell them, they're cutting you a check right now."

"I don't believe a damn bit of it," Rex said. "But just so I can have a good laugh, lemme see that letter."

Jack started to stand until Rex leveled the gun and said, "Sit down, squirrel."

He sank back onto the couch. "You want the letter,"

Jack said, "it should be on top of the desk."

Rex glanced down. "I don't see nothin'."

When Jack remembered where he had left it, he had the feeling of taking a punch to the gut. "Oh, fuck," he muttered.

"You got a problem?"

"The letter was in my coat."

"Uh-huh?"

"My coat was in my truck."

"Which truck? The truck that's a pile of charcoal now? That truck?"

The two stared at each other. Rex said, "I bet next you're gonna shit a turd in my hand and tell me it's a gold nugget."

"They'll pay you," Jack said.

Rex slid the chair back, walked to the couch, and stood over him. "You got any other con jobs to pull?"

"Call the man I was working for," Jack said. "Cactus Bloodworth. He's the one they sent the letter to. He'll tell you the same thing. Find out the real truth before you do something you'll regret."

"I might do somethin'," Rex said, "but I doubt I'll regret it."

"Call Cactus Bloodworth," Jack said. "I've got his number. Call him right now. He'll tell you."

Rex turned to the other man. "Now he wants me to make a phone call. What you think of that?" The man coughed an answer. Jack looked that way, a mistake. He didn't see Rex's gun swinging for him until it was too late to react.

The blow struck him below his left ear, hard enough to

knock him over. He was only down a few seconds when he felt himself being lifted upright by his hair. "Sit up, squirrel," he heard Rex say. "You got some work to do."

Jack put his hand to his ringing ear and came back with blood. Hot blades of pain made it hard to focus. "Listen up," Rex said as he walked back to Jack's desk. "Here's what you're gonna do." He began to pick through the papers on the desk. "Soon as I find us a blank sheet, you're gonna write somethin' for me. Soon as I—well, lookie here."

Rex picked up a sheet of paper, holding it at full arm's length, pinching a corner between thumb and forefinger. "What do you think I found?" He put that sheet down and held up another one of the copies of Loyce Slapp's surveillance reports. "Settin' right here on your desk in front of me the whole time," Rex said. "Like I tole you, I knew exactly why you wanted to get me out in that alley. Now I got the proof. You wanted to find out if I had the goods on my wife havin' a diddle with Bobby Slater."

The second man coughed again. Jack looked quickly at him. "Hey, how about that, squirrel?" Rex smiled. "I mention Bobby Slater and you look at him. You think that's Bobby, don't you? Don't you?"

Jack wasn't sure what he thought. He said nothing. Rex didn't wait for an answer anyway. "How'd you feel if I told you you was right? All this chasin' around for Bobby Slater that you did, and I've had him the whole time. I'd feel damn stupid if I was you, but then I ain't you, and thank the good Lord for that."

The man coughed three times. He had yet to say a word. Rex, still holding his gun, moved to the man's side and put a hand on his shoulder. "So may I present to you, squirrel, Mr. Bobby Slater."

Jack waited. Rex said, "Hey, you don't believe me? Shit, I got proof. Show him your driver's license, Bobby." The man stuck his gloved hand in his back pocket and pulled out a brown wallet. He flipped it open to display a license behind a clear plastic window.

"Well, there you go," Rex said. "Now that picture don't flatter him—hell, it don't even look like him, really—but we'll get a new one made. Won't we, Bobby?"

The man nodded, coughed, hawked, and stood to spit in a trash can. The wallet went back in his pocket.

Jack watched as the man began to tug at the fingers to remove his gloves. The left one came off first, then the right.

Jack stared at the man's right hand, and everything became clear.

The middle finger was missing. Mingo No-Bird, dead man walking. For Jack it was like taking another whack to the head. "You're Mingo Gideon," he said.

"Oh, shit, Mingo, he done snapped to it." Rex cackled. "The way your face looks right now, squirrel. What a fuckin' picture that would make."

Rex laughed some more. "All this runnin' around you did, squirrel, all these questions you just *had* to ask, and you never figured out it was really Bobby fuckin' Slater that I tossed in the lake? That it's really Bobby's ashes in the can?" Rex whistled. "Damn, I'm good."

34

If he tries anything stupid, Rex had told Mingo as he handed over the gun, just up and shoot the boy. Then Rex had said, You hear that? Try anything stupid and Mingo gets to shoot you. Telling the squirrel, Now get to work, you got a letter to write. A letter informing the Continental Centurion company that everything was clean as a whistle as far as the Rex Echols claim was concerned. Rex wanted it done by the time he returned. And I'll be back in under an hour, Rex had said when he walked out the door, maybe less if things go the way they're supposed to.

After that Rex had gone downstairs to Greenie's 24-HR. No sense in letting the squirrel know what was up. He had used the restaurant's pay phone to call Miss Sally's house. When she answered—no question it was her—Rex lowered his voice to say wrong number, then hung up. Thinking, Last phone call you'll get, hon.

Now he parked Mingo's heap of an Oldsmobile down the block from 3585 Normandy and checked a slip of paper, a note he had made from his files at the Melon Patch: Miss Sally lived in Apartment Number 3. Rex patted his jacket pocket and felt the outline of his penlight and his knife. He got out of the car and walked along the sidewalk, singing to himself as he went:

She can't fill your shoes, there's just no way.
But she sure looks great in your lingerie.

The bottom two apartments at 3585 were dark. Rex climbed the porch stairs to Number 3. A light glowed behind the curtains.

He leaned his shoulder against the front door, ready to shove his way in as soon as Miss Sally cracked it open. His knife was in his right hand. Rex tapped on the door, waited for an answer, got none, and tapped again.

He stepped to the window next to the door. With his pocketknife, a brand new Spyderco with a four-inch blade, he sliced away the screen. The window was unlocked, and it slid open with ease. Like telling him, Come on in. So he did.

A lamp was on in the living room, but he could see no light in the back. Rex stayed still for a good minute, listening for movement, hearing nothing. He flicked his penlight on and made his way down the hall.

He found her in the bedroom. Rex shined the penlight on her, letting the dim, frayed circle of yellow play over her for a moment. She was in the bed, on her stomach, asleep. Her hair was wrapped in a towel whose corner fell across her face.

He stood beside the bed and listened to her breathe.

The knife was in his gloved hand, the light in his mouth now like a cigar. Rex mounted the bed and sat on her, straddling her back. One hand gripped her hair through the towel. He pulled her head back. The other hand swung the knife. The blade flashed and he drew it across her throat.

There was a sucking and gurgling sound. Her body thrashed and bucked against his weight and then she was still. Rex used the towel to clean his knife as a black pool grew on the pillow.

He climbed off the bed and pulled the covers from the body. It was nude. Rex gripped one arm and one knee and rolled the body onto its back. He held a wrist, checking for a pulse like a nurse, and shined his weak light on her neck. The slash was shaped like a grin.

Rex moved the light to her chest to look for breathing. The small spot fell on a red rose. "Oh no," he whispered. Rex put the light on her face, his mouth forming the word but no sound coming out: April.

35 Sally drove south on Greenville Avenue, thinking about April, not sure why. Right after Sally got the wrong-number call, April had come from the bathroom, just out of the shower, towel around her wet hair, heavy-lidded, walking like a zombie, complaining of a splitting headache. Muttering that it was a hell of a way to spend her night off, but she'd had almost no sleep in two nights, and this one would be different. I've taken two of my little pills, she had said, and now I'm gonna have me a shot of cognac, turn out all the lights, and crawl into bed. Good thing you don't plan to come back tonight, she had told Sally, 'cause this bed'll be occupied. Nothing'll wake me up.

Sally had asked April if maybe two pills with liquor wasn't too much. Unless it puts me to sleep, April had said, then too much ain't enough. She was taking the cognac with her to the bedroom when Sally kissed her on the cheek and left.

Now, after a stop for gas, Sally looked for a parking

spot beneath the blinking green frog. She found one and pulled her car in. The plate-glass door was unlocked, as Jack had said it would be. She climbed the stairs of Greenie's Office Building, turned down the hallway, and saw the door to Suite Number Two cracked open. "Jack?" she said. She pushed on the door, leaned in, and saw someone coming at her.

It had taken Jack five minutes to unplug the Elvis lamp, working with his feet on the floor socket beneath the desk, doing it slowly and quietly so Mingo wouldn't notice. Sit your sorry ass here, Rex had said before he departed, pushing a chair for Jack to the side of the desk. Now, Rex had barked, write that damn letter. He had said it like a pissed-off dad ordering his kid to do his homework.

Rex left Mingo on the couch. Jack wrote, using a ballpoint pen on letterhead stationery, and worked at the lamp plug with his feet. Mingo still had not spoken, which was fine with Jack. He was listening for something else.

The stairway at the entrance to Greenie's Office Building had been nailed together sometime during Ike's first term. Enough pairs of feet had gone up and down it that each step sloped gently toward its center. A carpet runner muffled the comings and goings, but the sixth and eighth steps from the bottom still creaked when any adult put weight on them.

Jack, at his desk, heard the steps. He kept the pen moving but reached for the base of the lamp with his free hand. When Sally pushed open the door Jack yelled, "Run!" He sent the King sailing toward Mingo's head at the same time.

At the sound of Sally's voice, Mingo jumped from the couch and lunged toward her. Jack tried to match the lamp's flight path to Mingo's motion. The last time he had gone for Mingo's head, with the pipe at the Heart-o-the-Pines, Jack had thrown behind him. This one hit the target.

Elvis's head shattered across the side of Mingo's face. Mingo fell into Sally and they both went to the floor. Jack grabbed a golf club, a nine iron, from the bag in the corner. He raised the club as he moved toward the tangle of bodies.

Jack stopped when he saw the gun in Mingo's hand with its barrel against Sally's jaw. Mingo was smiling up at Jack, showing teeth that were crooked and gray. He spoke, his voice like the rusty, spitting water that comes from a tap long out of use. "I wouldn't," he said.

Mingo had them face down on the floor amid the pieces of the broken lamp. Jack's head was at Sally's feet. Their wrists were bound behind them with duct tape from Jack's supply cabinet. Mingo had wrapped their ankles as well. Jack had tried to talk to him until Mingo rasped, "Shut up or I tape your mouth."

They had been listening to Mingo cough for about fifteen minutes when Rex came up the stairs hard enough to make the floor tremble beneath them. He threw open the door, banging it against the wall. "Had to get fuckin' cute," he said. "Just had to, didn't you?"

Jack couldn't see him but heard his boots on the floor. The footsteps stopped and Rex said, "Look what you done, Miss Sally. You got all mixed up in this and April had to pay for it."

"Don't you hurt April," Sally said.

"Hey, it's *done*. All your little games—"

"Leave her alone," Jack said.

The steps came toward Jack. Sally said, "What'd you do to April? Don't you touch her. You hear me? You stay away from April. Do anything to her and you'll answer to me."

Rex took Jack by the hair again, pulling his head back to look him in the face. "All the way back over here, squirrel, I thought about what I was gonna do to you. I ast myself, Do I use the gun or the knife?"

Sally said, "Did you hear me? You don't touch April. I'm talking to you, Rex, you dimwit. You stay away from her."

Rex tried again with Jack. "Like I was about to say, squirrel, I couldn't decide whether—"

"If you hurt April," Sally said, "I'll cut off your balls and feed them to the ducks."

"That does it." Rex let go of Jack's hair. "Mingo? You got any more of that tape? Use some to shut Miss Sally up."

"Leave her alone," Jack said again. He heard the ripped-fabric sound of the tape being pulled from the roll, then Sally was quiet.

"Try this one more time." Rex was kneeling close to him. "Like I was sayin', squirrel. I couldn't decide whether to use the gun or the knife on you. Then I thought maybe just stompin' you would give me the most satisfaction." He prodded Jack's cheek with the tip of his boot. Jack could smell leather, polish, and dirt. "Then I thought about it some more."

Rex walked away. He seemed to be talking to Mingo

now. "I don't wanna leave a mess here. We probly got our fingerprints on stuff and there's pieces of paper with our names on 'em. We do it here, there'll be lots of people with lots of questions come to poke around. It's not worth it."

"So whadda we do?" Mingo asked in the rusty voice.

"Well . . . " Rex paused. "First thing, let me gather up ever paper I can find that has anything to do with you and me. While I'm doin' that, you tape 'em up a little better. Extra tight on squirrel."

"Can do."

"Then," Rex said, "let's go for a ride."

Mingo took Sally and Rex took Jack, the four of them going down the stairs and out the back exit. With their ankles taped, Sally and Jack had to hop down each step like children at play. "Do one thing stupid," Rex had told Jack as he hobbled along the hallway, "and she gets nailed."

A car was parked just outside the door. Jack didn't even notice what kind. All he saw was the open trunk lid. Mingo forced Sally into the back seat, and told her to lie down and stay that way.

Rex put the gun barrel to Jack's ear. He said, "Get in the trunk, squirrel." Jack squirmed in, his hands still bound behind him. He lay down amid a few blocks of two-by-four, a set of jumper cables, a towing chain, and a couple of empty antifreeze jugs.

The lid slammed shut, and all was black. Jack tried to breathe deeply, to keep the panic from welling up and taking him over. He felt as if he were in a trial-run coffin.

Jack heard the engine fire and the muffler rumble. The

taillights came on and cut the darkness, giving everything in the trunk the color of a bad sunburn. His face rested against a wet spot on the carpet—a good sign, Jack thought. If water could get in, so could air.

After some starts and stops, one bump bad enough to knock Jack's head against the lid, and an acceleration that threw him to the rear wall, they seemed to be on the freeway. The car's speakers, their undersides a couple of feet from his head, blared country oldies. Kenny Rogers and Johnny Cash, with ads for laxatives and interstate highway truck stops. He could smell the oily rags and the rubber of the spare tire. Over the music he could hear Mingo's muffled coughs. The car chugged along smoothly, the execution express.

There had been other times when Jack had thought he was about to die, but never had he been given so long to think it over. He began to see, again, courtroom photographs of the dead.

You looked at them one way, Jack thought, and the bodies in the pictures were the same as the empty shell of the katydid or the abandoned skin of a snake. Someone had used them, then went somewhere else, some other way. The flesh became molecules thrown back into the grab bag.

But one face kept coming back to him, that of a pizza deliveryman named Ellis Jones. Five or six years had passed since Jack had prosecuted the case. He saw the picture now as if he held it in front of him.

The photograph was taken at night, the flash beating back darkness for an instant. Ellis Jones, a black man in his thirties, had been found in a heap, one leg bent behind him as if made of rubber. He lay face up, eyes open in a dead stare at the bridge from which he had been thrown.

Ellis Jones was intercepted on his pizza delivery rounds by one Devron Tremont, eighteen, and Devron's seventeen-year-old running buddy, Arcell Rollison. As Arcell later testified, they forced Ellis Jones to drive his car to the Continental Avenue Bridge, over the Trinity River. Ellis Jones gave them all his pizza money and his one credit card, and said it was fine with him if Devron and Arcell took his car.

As they stood at the bridge railing Ellis Jones pleaded for his life. If you kill me, Ellis Jones said to them, my boy loses his father. He didn't really beg for himself, Arcell said: Dude just kept saying, My boy's just three years old. Asking us, Look over there in the car, see his picture taped to the dashboard.

Devron Tremont listened to it all, then shot Ellis Jones in the throat. Devron and Arcell tossed the body from the bridge. It dropped sixty-five feet into some tall riverside grass, where the cops took the photograph that Jack couldn't get out of his head.

Ellis Jones's wife and son were in court, front row, every day of Devron Tremont's trial, which made the jury want to give Devron the juice personally. When Arcell Rollison told how Ellis Jones had begged for his life, Jack looked at the picture of the dead man, then turned to see his son. They had the same face.

Now Jack thought of them both and worked at the tape on his wrists. He pushed and pulled for what seemed like an hour, finally stretching it enough to free a hand. Minutes later the car slowed, stopped, started, and stopped again. The lights died and the trunk went black.

Jack heard the gas cap being screwed off, some metallic banging, and the sound of gas draining into the tank. He moved as far forward as he could. "Sally?" he said, then louder, "Sally? Are you there?"

"Shut up." Rex's voice.

"I can't breathe in here," Jack said. "I need some air." Thinking, if he could get them to crack the trunk he could make some commotion. "I need air."

"Good," Rex said.

The draining stopped, and the gas cap went back on. Jack began to pound on the lid. He shouted, "Let me out." Hoping for somebody at the next pump, maybe a retiree in plaid pants gassing up his Winnebago, someone sure to call the highway patrol about voices from a trunk.

Jack quit when the car started moving once more. Rex called out, "Nice try, squirrel."

He figured he had been in there at least two hours, maybe three, when the car seemed to leave the pavement. The shocks squeaked as they moved slowly over an irregular series of bumps. They were either crossing a field or traveling a dirt road. A few minutes later the car stopped.

The engine and radio cut off. Two of the car's doors were opened and slammed shut. A third opened, and Jack heard Rex say, "Come on, Miss Sally, get out."

Jack wriggled onto his back. He tried to draw his knees to his chest but didn't have enough room. He wanted to kick the trunk lid open as soon as he heard the key turn in the lock. Maybe the lid would hit Rex in the face and give Jack an opening to come out swinging with a piece of two-by-four. Not much of a plan, Jack thought, but it was all he had.

"Hey, squirrel." Rex's voice came from just outside the trunk, followed by a metallic banging on the lid. "You awake?" Jack didn't answer. He heard Rex say, "Get on over there with her." Then more banging on the trunk lid. Rex said, "That's my gun, son."

There was the sound of the key slipping into the lock. Jack gripped a two-by-four. Rex said, "Now listen up, squirrel. I'm gonna open up the lid in a minute. I imagine you got the tape off your hands and feet and you made up a plan for somethin' stupid. So here's the deal. I gave my knife to Mingo and made him to stand over there with Miss Sally. I tole Mingo if you don't come outta that trunk like a nice boy, he's to start carvin' her up like the Christmas turkey. Got it?"

The key turned and the lid drifted up. A flashlight shone in Jack's eyes. Rex said, "Mingo, you got that knife ready?" Mingo coughed a yes. Rex said, "Hear that, squirrel?"

Jack let go of the wooden block and climbed from the trunk. Rex was singing:

She don't go halfway when she wants to break hearts.
I'm talkin' about Lila, who's missin' some parts.
She's one-legged, one-armed, and even one-eyed.
She looks pretty good if you just see one side.

He stopped when Jack got both feet on the ground. "Turn around," Rex said. Jack blinked and squinted against the flashlight beam. They were in some sort of clearing. He could hear the wind in the trees but couldn't see them. He remembered photographs again, this time of the ones who had been found dead in what the newspapers always called a secluded area.

"Sally," Jack said, not knowing where to look. "Are you all right?"

"She gonna be hurtin' bad if you don't do what I tole you," Rex said. "Mingo, if this dumbshit don't turn around in two seconds, then you start slicin' and dicin'. The Mingo-matic, squirrel, how you like that? Not available in any store."

Jack shielded his eyes with his arm and looked for Sally. "One," Rex said, "two." Jack was shivering in the cold. He shuffled his feet slowly and turned. Rex said, "Hands behind you now," and wrapped his wrists with tape. It went around Jack's ankles, too, as Rex whistled. "There you go," he said when he finished. "Now, let's walk."

He and Rex went first, with Rex showing the way by pushing the back of Jack's neck with the gun barrel. Jack could hear Mingo's and Sally's feet behind them. The flashlight beam bounced in front of them. "You don't have to do this," Jack said, hobbling through grass. "You'll get your money. There's nothing we can do to stop it. The company's going to pay."

"Squirrel, the only reason I don't tape your mouth, too?" Rex pushed at his neck with the gun. "I wanna hear you whimper a little, and I get the idea you're workin' up to that."

"Sally didn't have anything to do with this. She's not involved with it one bit."

"That train's done left the station."

Something glinted in the light ahead of them. Jack stared as the beam played over a wall, a window, and a door about thirty feet away, a sight so sudden and unexpected that he thought at first he was imagining it. The light caught two horseshoes over the door. Rex had brought them to his house in Baggett.

37 Rex reached to unlock the door and pushed Jack inside when it swung open. Jack's bound feet caught on the threshold. He fell, twisting as he went down to land on his shoulder. Rex switched on a lamp and helped Jack up by yanking on his hair. "Man, I love doin' that," Rex said.

Jack heard Mingo and Sally come in behind them. He tried to turn and look, but Rex stopped him with the gun. "Walk," Rex said, pushing him toward the rear of the house. They moved through the kitchen, out the back door, and into the darkness again. Rex reached toward the wall to flip a switch. The pool's underwater lights came on, and the water glowed blue-green.

Rex grabbed Jack's hair again, pulling him down. "On the floor," he said. Jack knelt on the patio's pebble and cement. Wavy light and shadow rippled over Rex as he gazed toward the far end of the pool and smiled. "Well, look what the cat drug in. What's shakin', hon?"

Sitting in a plastic chair in a dim corner was Baby Echols.

Her purse and some beer cans cluttered the table next to her. Baby wore the red jogging suit that Jack remembered. Even in the poor light he could see her frightened eyes. She stood and said, "What is this? I don't get this." Sally came onto the patio but not into the light. Mingo positioned himself behind her. "Who's that?" Baby said, trying to see. "What's goin' on?"

"You know, Baby," Rex said, "have to call it a big surprise to find you here, but I'm damn glad you showed up. Now you get to watch what happens when, A, you can't keep your fuckin' pants on—although I got to say, that worked out pretty good for me—and, number two, what happens when you can't keep your mouth shut. Lord knows what you told the squirrel, but you sure got him hot to trot on this whole deal. So what you see here"—Rex waved his gun toward Sally and Jack—"we can all chalk up to the stupid, stupid things Baby done. How you like that?"

Baby shook her head. "Rex, honey, I don't know what you're talking about."

Rex snorted and leaned down close to Jack. "Do you understand women? 'Cause I damn sure don't." He stood and looked back at Baby. "I'll take care of you in a minute. But first, friends . . . "

He got Jack by the hair again, pulling up, the gun barrel grinding into his ear. "I just had me a hell of a idea," Rex said. "Let's have us some fun. Mingo, bring Miss Sally over here so she can watch."

"What? Mingo?" Baby said as Mingo stepped out of the shadows. "*Mingo?*"

Rex laughed. "Old boy looks pretty good for a corpse,

242

don't he?" The watery light ghosted over Rex's face. He moved behind Jack and pushed him toward the pool. Saying, "You know, squirrel, I was thinkin' we'd come out here to Baggett, put a bullet in you, and bury you out in the woods where nothin'd ever find you but the worms. But then I thought, Hey, why not put a little more entertainment value into it? I mean, everybody likes a show."

They stood at the edge of the pool, next to a chrome ladder. Jack looked toward Baby. As loud as he could he said, "It was—" when Rex shoved him. Jack fell toward the big rectangle of blue-green water. The last thing he heard before he hit was Rex's laugh.

Tiny bubbles surged up around him as he sank. The water was warm. He pulled at the tape around his wrists, trying to stretch it or break it, but could feel nothing give. Rex had wrapped him tight. When Jack's feet touched bottom he crouched and sprang toward the silvery-black surface.

He gave a butterfly kick, all he could do with his ankles bound. His head broke the top of the water and he gasped for air. He heard Rex shout, "There she blows!"

Jack rolled onto his back and tried to float. He stayed up long enough to see Sally as she fought to free herself. Mingo had her by one arm and Rex the other. Her eyes locked with Jack's until his wet clothes dragged him back down.

He looked to the shallow end while sinking, and wasn't sure he could make it that far. Much closer was the ladder running halfway down the pool wall. He butterfly-kicked toward it.

Jack reached the ladder and got his feet on the bottom

rung, but without his hands he couldn't hoist himself up. The weight of his clothes pulled him backward. He angled out from the ladder like a man being imperfectly levitated.

He drew his feet back, righted himself, and kicked again. This time he got his chin over one rung and planted his feet on a lower one. He was in a crouch, his head still underwater, but ready to push himself up and try to catch the next rung with his chin. If he missed and fell he didn't think he would live. Jack was desperate to fill his lungs. Even water would be better than nothing.

Before he could move again he was being pulled up. Something had him by the hair. His face came out of the water. As he sucked in the air, let it out, and sucked it in again, he saw Rex smiling down on him.

"Hey, look what I caught," Rex said. "Beached squirrel."

Rex was on his knees. The hand with the gun hung over the ladder railing while the other gripped Jack's hair. Jack coughed. Rex said, "You're not as good as Ralph the Swimmin' Pig over to Aquarena Springs, but who is? Maybe you need more practice."

Jack could see Sally, struggling, held by Mingo. Baby was out of his sight line. "Tell your wife," Jack said as loud as he could, "who it was you really drowned."

"How about that, Baby." Rex looked up and over his shoulder. "Old squirrel here's gonna take his last dip and he's all worried about you."

"Ask him, Baby," Jack yelled. "Ask him who he really drowned. It was Bobby—" Rex plunged Jack's head into the water, then pulled him back out. When he cleared the surface Jack could hear Baby shouting, "What's he talking about, Rex?"

Rex looked at Jack and said, "Now you went and got her all curious."

Baby shouted, "What's he saying, Rex?"

Jack coughed hard, took some breaths, and said, "Big man, afraid of his wife."

"Afraid? Shit." Rex cocked his head her way. "Hey, Baby? It was your boyfriend, that little Bobby. I knocked him in the head and throwed him in the lake personally. With pleasure, I might add. How's that?"

He leaned close to Jack again. "How's that, squirrel? Good enough for you?" Then over his shoulder once more: "That's why, Baby, he ain't been around to honk your horn lately. His boners ain't what they used to be."

Rex laughed and came back to Jack with a big grin. "Well, let's see, where were we? We had plans for you to take another dip in the pool, seems to me ... But first, maybe a little Rex Echols composition to mark the occasion." He turned his head slightly and began to sing:

> *This is the last dance.*
> *This is your last chance*
> *To make a cheater outta me.*

Jack launched himself from the ladder. His mouth was open when his face hit the side of Rex's head. He clamped his teeth on Rex's ear.

As Rex screamed, the gun fell into the pool. Jack's weight pulled Rex toward the water. Rex clung to the ladder railing with one hand and punched Jack's face with the other. Jack squeezed his jaw tight while Rex screamed some more. He could taste blood.

Mingo started toward them. Jack saw Sally dive to the ground and Mingo tumble over her.

Rex took Jack's hair with one hand and yanked. With a guttural yelp Rex ripped his own head up and away. A ragged piece of ear hung from Jack's mouth, and the side of Rex's head bloomed red.

Jack spit out the ear. "This is the fuckin' end," Rex shouted. He still held Jack by the hair. Jack looked into a face that was twisted in rage and pain, with Rex staring back at him. The last eyes he would ever look into, the last person he would ever see.

Rex began to push Jack underwater. Baby came up behind Rex, put her gun to his head, and fired.

The sound of the shot echoed off the glass and bricks. Rex tumbled over Jack, into the pool. Jack lost his balance on the ladder and dropped underwater. One of Rex's arms drifted across Jack's face, with curled fingers softly raking his eyes.

Jack kicked away and turned to look. Rex was face down and sinking. There was a dime-sized hole just above where his ear used to be. Blood trailed from his head like red smoke.

The pool ladder nudged Jack's back. He was able to grasp the rail with one of his hands, get his feet on a rung, and caterpillar up, facing out. At the top he found Baby still holding her gun, the chrome-plated .22, gazing into the water after Rex. Sally lay on her side at the edge of the pool. Mingo was gone.

Jack struggled to his feet and hobbled toward Baby. "Put the gun down," he said. She raised her eyes to him and seemed surprised to find him there. "Put the gun down," he said again.

"He killed Bobby." She sounded as if she were talking in her sleep. "That's what he told me. He said he killed Bobby."

Jack called to Sally, "Are you okay?" She nodded yes. "Where's Mingo?" he asked. Sally moved her head toward the house. Jack turned back to Baby. "Listen to me. Put the gun on the ground. Then take this tape off my wrists. Go ahead, do it, Baby. Put the gun down."

Baby looked at the gun, blinked a few times, and placed it at her feet. "Here," Jack said, twisting and showing her his wrists. "Get this off me."

When his hands were free, he pulled the tape from his ankles, picked up the gun, and ran to Sally. Next to her was a small puddle of blood, black in the dim light, with a trail of drops leading to the house. He took the tape from her mouth. "What happened?" he said.

She had to take two quick breaths before talking. "I think he fell on his knife."

Jack unwrapped her wrists and ankles. "Stay here with Baby," he told her. Rex's flashlight lay on the patio floor beside the back door. He picked it up and entered the house.

He had the flashlight in his left hand and the gun in his right, trying to follow the trail of drops, ready to do a room-to-room. Jack gave up that plan when he heard a car cranking. As he ran out the front door, the engine fired to life. He saw the car make a half-circle in the field and then pull away down the unpaved drive toward the highway. The unlatched trunk flew open as it went, its interior light blinking as the lid bounced up and down.

The woods soon swallowed the light and the noise.

Mingo No-Bird had made his escape. Jack stood in the dark and thought, Maybe it's better that way.

By the time he got back to the pool Rex's body had settled on the bottom. "Come here," he said to Baby and Sally. He put his arms around both of them, hugging them, trying to stop their shaking. The three of them looked down on Rex.

"Well, now," he said. "Do we go or do we stay?"

"What are you saying?" Sally asked.

Jack released the hug. "I'm asking do we run, or do we call the law? Which in this case is Sheriff Loyce Slapp."

"Not him." Sally shook her head. "You can't call him. Not after what I heard Rex say in the car."

"Tell me," Jack said, "and we'll see."

Before he answered the doorbell, Jack walked to the edge of the pool and tossed Baby's gun in. It had taken Wayne Ambrose, chief of the Baggett Volunteer Fire Department, about twenty minutes to climb out of bed and drive to Rex Echols's house. Jack said he was sorry he had to call at such a late hour. "No problem at all," Wayne said. Jack, holding an ice pack to the welts on the side of his face, took Wayne to the pool. "My lord," Wayne said. "What the heck happened? How long's he been down there?"

"About an hour." Jack started back to the house. "I'm going to phone the Sheriff's Department now. I just wanted you to be around when they got here."

The teenage deputy who chewed tobacco arrived first, blue and red lights flashing on his patrol car. He took one look at the pool, spit brown juice into his styrofoam cup, and radioed the dispatcher to wake up Sheriff Slapp.

This time Loyce Slapp wore blue jeans and a black sweatshirt, and his hair still had the look of being mashed against a pillow. He walked in the house with his right wrist resting across the grip of his holstered gun. Justice of the Peace Webb Carroll followed him in, a camera hanging from his neck and his poodle cradled in one arm.

In clothes still damp, Jack led them out the back door. Webb Carroll studied the body in the water, stroked the dog's head, and said, "Uh-oh, look at that, Jim Dandy."

The sheriff stared down at Rex Echols. Jack could see the muscles on the side of Loyce Slapp's face tighten and release, then saw him close his eyes for a couple of seconds and lick his lips. He was breathing fast for a man standing still.

"We need some pictures, Webb," the sheriff finally said. Webb Carroll took a couple of shots from where he stood, not bothering to put Jim Dandy down.

Loyce Slapp turned to his deputy. "Fish him out."

The deputy blinked a few times. "Do what, Sheriff?"

"Goddamnit, get in there and get him. Don't make me tell you again."

The deputy began to undress. Wayne Ambrose said, "I'll help you get it." The two men stripped to their underwear and plunged into the pool. Loyce Slapp watched them, moving only once, when he turned to point at Jack, Sally, and Baby. "You three stay right there," he said.

Wayne Ambrose and the deputy pulled the body to the shallow end, then dragged it up the pool steps and onto the patio. It lay face up, water draining out of the clothing. "Webb, give me another picture," Loyce Slapp said.

Webb Carroll shot two frames from the same spot and

sank into a chaise lounge with a heavy sigh. The poodle rested on his lap. Loyce Slapp crouched next to Rex.

Jack told Sally and Baby, "Be right back." He walked to the body and said, "I guess it only takes one shot when you put it there."

The sheriff raised his face. His eyes were narrow and he talked as if his jaw were wired shut. "Get back over where I told you. I'll talk to witnesses in a minute."

"You can talk to me. That's all you'll need."

Loyce Slapp stood. "I'm about to make some arrests. Maybe three of them."

Jack smiled. "Save you some time, Sheriff. I'll solve the case for you on the spot." He stepped closer. "I know all about what happened. I know how Rex killed Bobby Slater and said it was Mingo."

The mud-colored eyes went from Jack to Rex and back to Jack. "I was right. You *are* crazy."

Jack leaned down into Loyce Slapp's face, and dropped his own voice. Two guys shouting at each other with whispers. Jack said, "You're trying to figure out how you can charge one of us with shooting Rex, aren't you? You do that, and it all comes out, Sheriff, every bit. I'm talking about your role in this whole thing."

"You've got nothing."

"I've got plenty." Jack ran it through his head: everything that Sally heard Rex say in the car. Then telling himself, If you knew just enough, and knew how to bluff, they'd always think you knew a lot more. He gestured with an open hand toward the body. "Old Rex here? He wrote everything down. Hey, Sheriff, the way you came up with this scheme, told Rex how it would work? Rex was taking notes."

"That's a lie."

Sure it's a lie, Jack thought, but now I'm going to make it true. He shook his head. "Every night you spent with April, Rex wrote it down. And remember when you showed up and shook him down for more money? Two hundred thousand, wasn't it?" With Jack thinking, That's what Sally said. "Am I wrong about that, Sheriff, two hundred grand? Well, it's all on paper, and I've got it in a safe back in Dallas." It was going so well that Jack added more. "But that's not the worst part. It's all on tape, too. Rex had a machine going on you the whole time. Those tapes? I got them in the same safe."

Loyce Slapp swallowed, licked his lips, and seemed to shrink. "You try to lock me up," Jack said, "or you touch either one of these two women, guess what our attorney shows to anybody and everybody, first thing? Lots of people'll be interested in Rex's stuff. In his notes and tapes starring Sheriff Loyce. I'm thinking hometown folks, newspapers, federal grand juries . . . "

The sheriff's eyes looked glassy. Jack said, "Now stay with me, 'cause here's where I solve it for you. Rex killed himself. Committed suicide, case closed. Rex stood in front of me, Sally, and Baby and shot himself right in the head."

He pointed a finger just above his ear and pulled an imaginary trigger. "Ka-boom," Jack said. "Nothing we could do to stop it . . . You know, people said Rex hadn't been the same since the drowning. I guess he was overcome by grief."

Loyce Slapp stared at the body and sagged. "You try to sink me," Jack said before he walked away, "and I take you down, too."

252

39 Jack drove Baby's red Prelude. Sally sat beside him, with Baby curled on the back seat, asleep. They were an hour outside Dallas, on I-30, at four in the morning. A light rain fell. Jack said to Sally, "You can't blame yourself."

"I'm the reason April's dead."

"No," Jack said, "*Rex* is the reason April's dead."

Jack had telephoned Sally's apartment from the house in Baggett. Sally stood beside him as he dialed, both of them watching through the window as Rex Echols's body was bagged up and hauled away. "She'll answer," Sally said. "She has to."

After two rings a man picked up. Jack asked for April and the man wanted to know who was calling. Jack identified himself and asked, Who's this? Turned out it was Bill Leonard, a cop whose cases Jack had prosecuted a couple of times. A homicide detective. Jack looked at Sally and shook his head.

On the phone Jack played dumb, asking Leonard in a

friendly way what the hell he was doing there, was he hanging with April?

Leonard wouldn't say anything until he had Jack's whole story: How Jack and Sally had gone to East Texas overnight to see a friend, leaving April at Sally's. April hadn't been feeling too well, Jack said, so they were calling to check on her.

You call a sick friend, Leonard said, at this time of night? Jack answered, What's wrong with that? Adding, Bill, come on, what's going on there, anyway?

Leonard told him that a neighbor couple, coming home, had seen someone leaving in a hurry, acting strange, talking to himself. A short, stocky white man, Leonard said, with a cowboy hat. Asking Jack, That ring any bells? No bells with me, Jack said.

The neighbors went upstairs, where they found a ripped screen and a raised window. When no one answered their knocks they called the police. It's a holy mess in that bedroom, Leonard told Jack.

Now, in the car, Jack turned to Sally. "The cops'll probably have a composite sketch, if the witnesses got a good enough look. They'll want to know if anyone might have wanted to hurt you or April. Any suspicious phone calls, Peeping Toms, that kind of thing."

Sally looked out her window at the dark fields and smoked. "I never thought it would happen like this."

"I'll be with you if they let me. At the police station, I'm talking about. What you need to do is answer no to everything. Tell them you can't ID the sketch, you don't know why anyone would kill April or come hunting for you."

"I should have known."

"Are you listening to me, Sally? Don't slip away."

She faced him. "Two of my friends are dead. Maybe I couldn't do anything about Bobby. But April . . . "

"I know that. I'm sorry. I feel responsible, too. I played my part in it. But it's done. You need to keep a clear head and think about where we are now."

"Yeah?" she said, turning away, voice full of sharp edges. "Where are we now?"

"Rex got what he deserved. He's the guy who killed your friends, and he's taken care of. And you can be sure Mingo won't be coming back, even if he survives the knife wound. He's officially dead, remember? If he turns up he has to start explaining why. What's he gonna say, he was reincarnated? As for the sheriff, we've got him by the balls. Or at least he thinks we do. That's the next best thing."

Sally smoked her cigarette and looked out the window, where there was nothing to see.

Jack said, "Don't forget Baby. If this whole thing unravels, Baby's a good bet to go to prison." He looked over his shoulder to see her still sleeping. "She saved our lives, Sally. Now you can save hers."

He waited until Sally turned to him. "I'm not saying it's perfect," he told her. "I'm not even saying it's good. But it's the best we've got."

They pulled in front of Greenie's 24-HR well before dawn. Jack parked under the blinking green frog and asked Baby, "You sure you don't want me to drive you home?"

She rubbed her eyes. "I'll be okay."

Jack opened the driver's door of the Prelude. "You call me if you need anything," he said before stepping out.

"I will."

"If somebody contacts you and you need a refresher on what to say or what to do, call me."

"Don't worry."

Jack and Sally stood on the sidewalk, watching Baby start her car and drive away. "She'll have some money now, anyway," Jack said. "She'll get the Mingo payment."

The plate-glass door to the Greenie's Office Building was still unlocked. Jack and Sally walked upstairs, not saying anything. In Jack's office the broken Elvis lamp lay on the floor. Jack's blood had dried into brown stains on the couch. He tried to hug Sally, but she turned from him. Her eyes had a stunned look. Jack stepped in front of her and gripped her shoulders. "Wherever you're pulling back to," he said, "don't do it. Something like this, we can help each other."

Sally broke from him. She'd feel a lot better, she said, if she could just wash her face. He watched her walk out the door and turn down the hall toward the rest room.

When she did not return in fifteen minutes Jack went to the women's room door and knocked. He got no answer. He stepped inside and found no one. He ran downstairs and looked for her car, but it was gone.

40 A few days after he returned from Baggett, Jack stood before a judge with his hands clasped behind him and pleaded guilty. He offered no excuses, made no plea for mercy.

The judge was a small, bald, wrinkled man named Reynolds who seemed about to disappear into his black robe. He sat on a high bench with a large American flag hanging on the wall behind him. Judge Reynolds slipped on a pair of bifocals and gazed at a sheet of paper, shaking his head.

"This is not clear." The judge looked over the top of his glasses at Jack. He had the kind of voice that came from a lifetime of smoking menthols. "I can't make sense of this. Somebody please tell me what the hell happened."

Jack cleared his throat. "Your Honor, I took a pair of scissors and cut off the ponytail of a guy who was harassing me."

The judge stared at Jack over the bifocals, blinked a few times, nodded, then cut loose with a couple of laughs that dissolved into a coughing fit. When he got his wind back he turned to the prosecutor, an earnest, fresh face just out of law school. "Is the complainant present?" the judge asked.

The prosecutor scanned the courtroom quickly. "I don't think so, Your Honor."

"Too bad. I wanted to see what the pony looks like when he loses his tail. All right . . . " The judge uncapped a pen and signed a paper. "Thirty days probation. Next time, get your barber's license first."

The discovery of April's body had rated a ten-inch story inside the Metro section of the paper. The story identified her as Louise April McAllester, age thirty-one, a local waitress. Found by officers investigating a break-in. Police had made no arrests. Residents of the area were advised to keep their windows and doors locked.

A funeral notice appeared later in the week. Services were held in her hometown of Picayune, Mississippi. The only survivors listed were an aunt and an uncle. Jack sent flowers. He started to write a note, threw it away, then tried again. He didn't know April well, he said, but her friends had always said she was warm and good-hearted, and many people would miss her.

For three weeks he looked for Sally. Yellow police tape—CRIME SCENE DO NOT ENTER—still hung on her apartment door, and neighbors said they hadn't seen her. Jack spent hours sitting in the car his insurance company had rented for him, parked in the school lot across the street, waiting for her to come home. He tracked down her family in Texas City, but they hadn't heard from her in a month. Bill Leonard in homicide said she had been by once to look at the composite sketch, his only contact with her.

Cactus Bloodworth threw Jack a new case, and wondered after a few days why he wasn't doing more with it. He had dinner with his ex-wife, regular table. "You look lost," Kathy said.

On a Wednesday night Jack stayed at his office late because he didn't feel like going home. Around ten he walked down to Greenie's to have a cup of coffee and read the sports section for the second time. He was on his third cup when she slipped into the seat across from him.

"I've been out to Baggett," Sally said. Talking as if she'd seen him just that afternoon. "I went to the funeral home and claimed Bobby's ashes."

"The funeral home never knew it was Bobby."

"I told them I was Mingo Gideon's sister."

Jack watched her light a Merit and blow the smoke toward the ceiling. "The urn's in my car," she said. "I'm going to drive up to Oklahoma tomorrow and give it to Bobby's mother."

"That's a long drive to make by yourself."

"I've got plenty of time."

Jack sipped his coffee while Sally smoked. After maybe a minute he said, "You going to tell Bobby's mother the whole story?"

"As much as I can." Sally killed her cigarette in the ashtray. "She's his mother, so she needs to know." Sally raised her eyes to meet Jack's. "I could use some help if you feel like it."

"I feel like it." Jack was so happy to see her he almost started to sing.

BIG TOWN

Doug J. Swanson

'Jack Flippo. Just the right guy.'

Once the hottest young lawyer in the DA's office, now slumming it in a neighbourhood that went from bust to bust without the boom, Jack Flippo scrapes a living by snooping for Hal Roper, a seedy Dallas attorney. It's a bum deal but choice is a commodity in short supply, and when Hal needs someone to dabble in a set-up, a few thousand dollars, a little liquor and a lot of sex, he knows that Jack is just the right guy for the job.

'The dialogue is swift and punchy and the appalling characters are horribly believable. A very smooth debut; a writer to watch' *Sunday Telegraph*

'Detective fiction at its finest – fun, fast and full of surprises. The characters are exuberantly dirty, the dialogue is pricelessly funny and true' *Carl Hiaasen*

'Deliciously deadpan . . . Traditional in the sense that he reminds you of the very best (Dashiell Hammett in particular). But, in every important respect, original, engaging, funny and alert' *Literary Review*

FICTION
0 7515 1247 8

THE BODY FARM

Patricia Cornwell

Black Mountain, North Carolina: a sleepy little town where the local police deal with one homicide a year, if they're unlucky, and where people are still getting used to the idea of locking their doors at night.

But violent death is no respecter of venue, and the discovery of the corpse of an 11-year-old girl sends shock waves through the community, Dr Kay Scarpetta is called in to apply her forensic skills to this latest atrocity, but the apparent simplicity of the case proves something of a poisoned chalice – until Scarpetta finds enlightenment through the curious pathologists' playground known as the Body Farm . . .

From the award-winning author of *Cruel and Unusual*, a spellbinding new Scarpetta mystery that once again proves Patricia Cornwell's complete mastery of the genre.

'Cornwell . . . will find it difficult to better *The Body Farm*'
Marcel Berlins, *The Times*

'There are passages in Cornwell's novels which stop you in their tracks . . . [She] deploys prose like a scalpel'
Literary Review

FICTION
0 7515 1221 4

LIGHTS OUT

Peter Abrahams

Eddie Nye is about to wake up from a fifteen-year nightmare. Only to find that reality's no day-dream either . . .

Stepping back into the land of the free after fifteen years behind bars, Eddie Nye's first priority is to find the real criminals who should have served his sentence. For though he went to prison an innocent man, Eddie walks out with the knowledge that dog eat dog is the only way to survive.

The events that culminated in his arrest play constantly on his mind, but it is only after his release that Eddie begins to learn the truth behind his crime. And as he does, he finds himself at the centre of a second, much larger one, hatched in cell C-93 of the prison he left behind . . . a crime that is deeper and stronger than he can imagine, touching not only his life but also those closest to him. And above it all, there is the need for revenge: finding the man who robbed him of fifteen years of his life . . .

FICTION
0 7515 1144 7

☐	Big Town	Doug J. Swanson	£4.99
☐	The Body Farm	Patricia Cornwell	£5.99
☐	Lights Out	Peter Abrahams	£5.99

Warner Books now offers an exciting range of quality titles by
both established and new authors which can be ordered from
the following address:

    Little, Brown and Company (UK),
    P.O. Box 11,
    Falmouth,
    Cornwall TR10 9EN.

Alternatively you may fax your order to the above address.
Fax No. 01326 317444.

Payments can be made as follows: cheque, postal order
(payable to Little, Brown and Company) or by credit cards,
Visa/Access. Do not send cash or currency. UK customers
and B.F.P.O. please allow £1.00 for postage and packing for
the first book, plus 50p for the second book, plus 30p for
each additional book up to a maximum charge of £3.00
(7 books plus).

Overseas customers including Ireland, please allow £2.00 for
the first book plus £1.00 for the second book, plus 50p for
each additional book.

NAME (Block Letters) ....

....

ADDRESS ....

....

....

☐ I enclose my remittance for ....

☐ I wish to pay by Access/Visa Card

Number ☐☐☐☐☐☐☐☐☐☐☐☐☐☐☐☐☐☐

Card Expiry Date ☐☐☐☐